HOLIDAY

WALDO FRANK

Introduction by Kathleen Pfeiffe

T0307773

UNIVERSITY OF ILLINOIS PRESS
Urbana and Chicago

Introduction © 2003 by the Board of Trustees
of the University of Illinois
Holiday © 1923 by Boni & Liveright, Inc.
© renewed 1950 by Waldo Frank
Reprinted by arrangement with Liveright
Publishing Corporation
All rights reserved
Manufactured in the United States of America
P 5 4 3 2 1

♾ This book is printed on acid-free paper.

Library of Congress Cataloging-in-Publication Data
Frank, Waldo David, 1889–1967.
Holiday / Waldo David Frank ; introduction by
Kathleen Pfeiffer.
p. cm.
ISBN 0-252-07133-6 (pbk. : acid-free paper)
1. African-Americans—Fiction.
2. Southern States—Fiction.
3. Lynching—Fiction.
4. Racism—Fiction.
I. Title.
PS3511.R258H6 2003
813'.52—dc21 2002040931

HOLIDAY

CONTENTS

Introduction by Kathleen Pfeiffer vii

PART ONE: DUSK 9

PART TWO: DAWN 73

PART THREE: NOON 109

Interlude

PART FOUR: DUSK 187

INTRODUCTION

Kathleen Pfeiffer

Waldo Frank did not consciously seek to participate in the emerging "New Negro" movement of the 1920s when he took up the subject of lynching in *Holiday,* his sole fictional foray into African American culture. Yet his publisher, Boni & Liveright, placed him squarely in the middle of the movement when it advertised his novel in the March 1925 special issue of *Survey Graphic,*[1] titled "Harlem: Mecca of the New Negro," between ads for Jessie Redmon Fauset's *There Is Confusion* and Jean Toomer's *Cane.*[2] Thanks to the fickle nature of the American literary marketplace, few readers today are likely to have heard of *Holiday,* let alone Waldo Frank, yet his stature in 1925 ought not to be underestimated. Alan Trachtenberg notes that "at one time his name stood for the radical cultural and aesthetic aspirations of a whole generation of writers" ("Preface" viii), and for the majority of readers of the *Survey Graphic* special issue, Frank's name would have been by far the more familiar of the three.

To prepare himself to write *Holiday,* which depicts the events of a single day in the fictional southern town of Nazareth, culminating in the brutal lynching of the novel's central figure, John Cloud, Frank traveled to Spartanburg, South Carolina, with Toomer, with whom he had become friendly. Their correspondence clearly illustrates that the journey solidified an intimacy between them that both men treasured. "We understand each other in a way that is beautifully mysterious," Frank wrote (n.d., Toomer Papers). Toomer agreed that Spartanburg "gave us each other as perhaps no other place could" (n.d., Toomer Papers). They corresponded often and optimistically about the collaborative nature of their respective works and anticipated joint publication of the books they would write. Shortly before they departed for Spartanburg, Toomer told Frank, "I cannot think of myself as being separated from you in the dual task of creating an American literature, and of developing a public, however large or small, capable of responding to our creations. Those who read and know me, should read and know you" (2 Aug. 1922, Toomer Papers).

* * *

Waldo Frank was born into an upper-middle-class family in Long Branch, New Jersey, on August 25,

1889. His parents, Julius J. Frank and Helene Rosenberg Frank, maintained a cultured, privileged home in which music, literature, art, and imaginative expressions were highly valued. A nonobservant Jewish family, the Franks had four children, of whom Waldo was the youngest. As a boy, he exhibited a precocious intellect and often rebelled against authority, both at home and at school. He was expelled from the Horace Mann School for refusing to apologize to a teacher whose sculpture he had broken during a classroom scuffle, and he was not allowed to graduate from De-Witt Clinton High School because he refused to take a required Shakespeare course whose teacher, he believed, was underqualified. Julius Frank arranged for his son to attend Les Chaumettes Pensionnat in Lausanne, Switzerland, where he read French literature; later, Waldo earned B.A. and M.A. degrees from Yale University (the former in three years, the latter in one). "When he graduated in 1911," Michael Ogorzaly reports, "his two degrees were conferred together, and he was made an honorary fellow of the university and awarded a Phi Beta Kappa key" (19).

Peripatetic, imaginative, and curious, Waldo Frank journeyed to Wyoming, Montana, Chicago, New York, and Paris in the months following his graduation, revealing a restlessness that was typical of many in his generation. A member of the avant-garde in his writing, both public and private, his social activities, and his evolving spiritualism, he landed in Greenwich Village in the 1910s and became one of the new century's bohemians. Christine Stansell writes that these self-consciously modern rebels "made modernity local and concrete, tangible to a popular American audience":

> They created the first full-bodied alternative to an established cultural elite, a milieu that brought outsiders and their energies into the very heart of the American intelligentsia. They developed an unrivaled vision of feminism—with its powers to recast men's and women's lives—as a critical ingredient of modern culture. With intuitions and perceptions nurtured by experiments in the arts, they achieved distinct forms of sociability—in conversation, friendship, and sexual love—which they thought could carry the hopes of the age into the future. They injected into the politics of the left a new cultural dimension, as well as psychological identifications between working-class and middle-class people, that lent tremendous flexibility and originality to the popular politics of the era. (3)

Like them, Frank enthusiastically celebrated cultural pluralism as a way of redefining American national identity.

In 1916, Frank joined the critics James Oppenheim and Van Wyck Brooks as an associate editor of *The Seven Arts,* one of many new magazines dedicated to providing a forum for criticism, literary innovation, and other written expressions of the emerging modernist national spirit. *The Seven Arts,* which published just twelve issues (between November 1916 and October 1917) before losing its financial backing, cultivated writers whose political sensibilities reflected those of its editors. George Hutchinson notes the numerous resonant connections between *The Seven Arts* and the Harlem Renaissance and argues persuasively that the new magazines and publishers "transformed the cultural landscape and opened spaces for the emergence of African American literary modernism" (93).

Another of the intellectuals to influence Waldo Frank at this time was Margaret Naumberg, a New Yorker born in 1890. Like Frank, Naumberg was exceptionally gifted and privileged. She earned a B.A. degree from Barnard College in 1912, studied with John Dewey, and was one of the first Americans to train with Maria Montessori, the Italian physican and educator. Naumberg and Frank met around 1914 and married in 1916. Theirs was a union based on mutual respect, friendship, and intensely reciprocal support, though it was not monogamous.

During her marriage to Frank, Naumberg founded the Walden School (later called the Children's School), which took a revolutionary approach to education through employing psychoanalytic principles. She also introduced her husband to Freudian psychoanalysis, which merged with the numerous other influences—spiritual mysticism, realism, political radicalism, a decided rejection of cultural materialism—that already informed his writing. This iconoclastic blend of philosophies, together with an elliptical and unconventional writing style, became the hallmark not only of fiction such as *Holiday* but of his nonfiction cultural critiques, such as *Our America,* the 1919 work that Ann Douglas describes as "a pioneering attempt to psychoanalyze American culture" (67–68). Psychoanalysis alone does not account for *Our America*'s complexity, however. In its condemnation of the Puritan legacy of repression, its celebration of pioneer spiritual power, and its exaltation of Walt Whitman's vision of multitudes, *Our America* calls for artistic and social revolution. Frank's own bitter detachment from "his" America is evident in his later autobiographical account of this time (written in the third person):

> The post-World-War in which Frank willed to be both man-of-letters (who can be bred only within a stable social order) and judge and smiter of that order was the America of Warren Gamaliel Harding, champion of "normalcy," to which he fondly hoped to "turn America back"; and of Calvin Coolidge whose proud word was: "the business of America was business." Emerson and Thoreau would have agreed—and wept. There were no tears in the people. Liquor had been denied them by constitutional amendment so that they might soberly contemplate their glories and powers. . . . H. L. Mencken and Sinclair Lewis sneered at them as

> "yokels" and the "boobosie," but these louts and their prim-lipped wives had inherited the earth. (Ts., Frank Papers, n.p.)

Sigmund Freud's theories of the subconscious and of human psychology allowed modernists to escape what they saw as the strictures of narrow, Puritanistic, rational thought. The critical essays that comprise *Our America* accuse social institutions of inhibiting the American spirit and restricting the innate potential of the self-determining individual; Van Wyck Brooks called this book "'the Bible of our generation'" (*Autobiography* 87, qtd. in Hutchinson 106). If *Our America* indicates the bitter disappointment Frank felt in his culture's values, it also reveals his corresponding participation in and embrace of modernist culture and the avant-garde. Like many of his fellow modernist writers, intellectuals, and artists, he eschewed the theological and moral certainty of previous generations and lauded the revolutionary potential of blending such systems as Freudian psychoanalysis, spiritual mysticism, and communism. By embracing the Freudian concept of repression and discerning its destructive force in American culture at large, he and his contemporaries rejected the alleged neuroticism of their time.

Frank had long been drawn to Whitman (as a student, he won the gold medal in DeWitt Clinton High School's annual oration contest with a selection from

Leaves of Grass), and the poet influences the ideology presented in *Our America.* Frank was particularly taken by Whitman's sense of unity and wholeness in American democracy, and he called for his audience to seek out a similarly unified Being. Whitman, he argued, was a great mystic: "He saw the movements of men upon the flat planes of mundane life in its relation to all mundane life. He saw the unitary flow of all mundane life in its relation to an infinite Being of which it was an elementary part" (*Our America* 202). For Frank, as for Whitman, life's essence can be found in the quotidian: "We must begin to generate within ourselves the energy which is love of life. For that energy, to whatever form the mind consigns it, is religious. Its act is creation. And in a dying world, creation is revolution" (232).

The intellectual context provided by *Our America*'s nuanced critique of American culture helps us to distinguish *Holiday* from the other so-called Negro novels of the 1920s, a genre suspected of exploiting black culture by catering to the countless white readers who were fascinated by black America's supposedly spiritual and unrepressed essences. The most notorious of these novels was Carl Van Vechten's *Nigger Heaven,* but such black-authored fiction as Claude McKay's *Home to Harlem* also fell prey to the charge of pandering to the white audience's racist assumptions by focusing on risqué cabaret scenes and exuberant nightlife.

Frederick J. Hoffman noted in 1949 that in Frank's writings "this defiance of Puritan morality acquired the characteristics of a primitivism, an attempt to point out the great happiness of people who were not brought up in terror of sex and who therefore lived a normal, happy, casual life" ("Philistine" 252). Today's readers will determine for themselves whether such "primitivism" exists in *Holiday*'s black characters.

In his unpublished autobiographical writings about the 1920s, Frank adopted the technique for writing "Formulations"—a process of self-discovery advocated by the eastern mysticism of a Russian spiritualist named G. I. Gurdjieff and his follower, A. R. Orage, in which one examines one's life from a third-person point of view. Frank's involvement with Gurdjieff and Orage during the 1920s was brief and, as Casey Blake notes, "he broke with both men on the grounds that theirs was a spiritualism of withdrawal and retreat, rather than the militant creed of social transformation he had called for in *Our America*" (126). It is curious, then, that Frank employed rhetorical strategies of detachment, fragmentation, and withdrawal in describing this time of his life when all of his efforts sought unity. "That May in New York had been a poignant one: of joy and pain," he recalled of the months before he wrote *Holiday*. "In a hospital on Stuvysent [*sic*] Square, Waldo's wife Margaret, gave birth to her son and in another hospital uptown, the son of Waldo's brother, 7-year old Roger was dying of cerebral meningitis. Waldo swung from one to the other: the place of life, the place of death, aware of the balance and unity between them. The episode revealed the whole human story as of a single creature covering the earth; reaching invisible antennae toward sky beyond sky and toward earth beneath earth" (Ts., Frank Papers, n.p.).

This account, written around 1963 or 1964, gives a sense of the complex personal and familial pressures facing Frank as husband, father, brother, uncle, and writer. It also reflects his desire for unity and his predisposition toward understanding life as a struggle between opposing forces. A crossed-out passage from the typescript makes this clear: "Here, in the young philosopher poet at ease before his open hearth revising the rhythms black and white of *Holiday,* lived inner contradiction that was going to cause trouble" (n.p.). An intense and passionate man, Frank wrote as he experienced life: as antinomies of success and pain, failure and pleasure. One might argue that this character trait was borne out by the legacy of his three marriages, numerous novels, extensive political work, and considerable travel—an unending search for the wholeness and unity that constantly eluded him.

Waldo Frank had long been concerned with women's roles in society, and he may well have been endeavoring to engage some of these concerns in *Holiday* through his depiction of the female protagonist, Virginia Hade. "Woman will overcome her present unadventurous attitude toward life, because it is, with her awakening mind," he wrote around the time he was plotting the novel. "The intellectually courageous but emotionally timid woman will disappear. She fails to function either in the free or the slave portion of society. She fails, i.e. and dies" (Notebook VIII, 8). Echoing the constricted social systems of the American past, he viewed the American woman's position in terms of Puritanistic repression and advocated "a new chastity, a new family tie . . . based on experience + conviction . . . rather than the rejection of experience and the accidental of causality, as today" (ibid.).

Frank's extensive discussion of woman's state may reflect his own ambivalence about marriage and family (the previous entry in his notebook, for instance, reveals that "'having a baby' is particularly painful mechanics since *you* are but an inconscient [*sic*] part of the machine. Your spirit that cares to refocus all life to itself as center is bruised and offended and not a little marred by its failure to do so here . . . where life so clearly enters outside the pale accessoriship [*sic*] of Father" [Notebook VIII, 7]). But it also speaks to modernism's rejection of sexual conventions. His critique of gender roles employs the language of slavery, a conflation of race and sex that *Holiday* maps through Virginia Hade's complex relationship with John Cloud. Likewise, *Holiday* engages the network of influences and pressures that sustain such conventions, illustrating Frank's belief that "man, however far he be individually evolved, can't be free . . . since obviously the sexual act involves a community of reaction as well as a community of sense" (ibid., 10).

Frank maintained notebooks of his work's progress and professional plans throughout his life. The first mention of *Holiday* appears in Notebook VII, recorded in the spring of 1922. These early notes contain much of the impressionistic qualities that would shape the novel. For example: "*Opening:* The sun, reddening, . . . pines: in woods full of copper green glints + song + laughter: everywhere negroes + children calling, shouting. The determined gang of [. . .] whites, hear the music: it seems to mock them: pass occasional girls or boys—silent—. . . . The colored song they cannot touch" (69). Frank conceived of the tale as a "carnival story" and wrote to himself, "*Here*'s a *Magnificent Theme* for *Your Hand.* A study of life in a small Mississippi town . . . the gradual growth [of a] hidden passionate tumor = and its [. . .] Outbreak in 1) the negro's raping a girl and 2) the whole community's lynching [. . .] negroes. Holiday. Festival. Carnival" (70). *Holiday* was not just a trendy, 1920s Negro novel. From the start, Frank understood the racial construction of whiteness as well as blackness: "*Juxtaposed:* the *ugly* huddled 'white' town of frame houses, . . . trees cut down: white wood [. . .] *niggertown*—timberland of sparse pine, live oak, [. . .] + paintless shanties" (70).

The opening inscription of Notebook VIII, begun on May 1, 1922, reveals the writer's frame of mind at the time. "There is no reason to worry or repine," Frank wrote. "Everything deep goes well. If you could but be satisfied with this—with the Deep, I mean. For look: you have elected to live and to work deep. The price of that is: what you elected to be! There are swift surface breakings. Would they seem such shattering waves to one living deep, indeed?" (1). This passage worries about the relationship between the surface (appearance) and depth (essence) of one's identity. Frank determined "failure" as an inability to "fuse into a Person," and he concluded that since he could not "become a whole surface Person," he would embrace the alternative, which was "to become a whole Deep Person" (1). The importance of these philosophical beliefs for our understanding of Frank's fiction is suggested in his published memoirs, where he explains that the "premise and matrix" of all his fiction was "the nature of the individual": "the premise for my work is that the individual is unreal and is transformed into truth, instantaneously, nonlinearly, *only* as the timeless and spaceless Presence speaks in him" (*Memoirs of Waldo Frank* 102).

Holiday's original title, "Carousal," evokes the grotesquely carnival atmosphere of a lynching. But as a northern urban Jew, Waldo Frank would necessarily have had a much different experience of lynching from that of southern African American writers such as James Weldon Johnson, who depicts lynching ironically in *The Autobiography of an Ex-Colored Man* (1912) and Langston Hughes, whose poem "Lynching Song" shows lynching to be a horrifying form of racialized social control. Indeed, Frank's notebook entries indicate that his concerns in the novel reached beyond a social critique of racism alone. "Two fears keep woman unchaste in her love: the morrow and the moral," he wrote (Notebook VIII, 11). A page later: "Enemies must have common ground. Else, they are not enemies but strangers" (12). Frank's life included only the most limited experience of having to negotiate racial identity and its social implications; indeed, the fact that he never suffered through segregation as a black man may lead readers to question the novel's authenticity.

Frank was one of many white modernists who pursued personal relationships and artistic collaborations with black writers. Recall Carl Van Vechten's well-known friendships with Langston Hughes, Nella Larsen, and James Weldon Johnson. Hart Crane and Sherwood Anderson also sought out the company of blacks, believing that their own writing and, indeed, their consciousness would benefit from such contact. "What white moderns like Hart Crane, Waldo Frank, and Sherwood Anderson hoped to get from their friendships with black moderns like Toomer," Ann Douglas explains, "was the Negro genius for religious feeling, the saving expressiveness that American Calvinism in their view had conspicuously lacked" (94). These were complex motives, to be sure, and today's readers may well be offended by the ostensibly fetishistic enchantment of these white writers with blackness. Thadious Davis highlights the exploitative undertones of Anderson's observation that "much beautiful stuff might be got" from black America (410), and Toomer's reservations about Anderson bear this out: "He limits me to Negro," Toomer complained in a letter to Frank (Dec. 1922, Toomer Papers). It is worth pointing out, however, that Toomer simultaneously distinguished Frank's racial and artistic sensibility: "No one in this country (which means the world as far as CANE is concerned) [understands me] but you my brother" (ibid.).

The brief yet intense friendship Frank shared with Toomer is an important part of the story of *Holiday*'s evolution. The two men met in 1919, during a trip to New York that Toomer devoted to establishing literary acquaintances. The grandson of a Reconstruction politician named P. B. S. Pinchback, Toomer was an ambitious apprentice writer, hungry for connections and an audience. His life until this time was characterized by apparently aimless wandering from one place to another, during which he held a number of jobs, attended several schools, and assumed a variety of names. He was captivated by *Our America*, particularly by its emphatic call for a revalued national identity. Following their first meeting, he wrote to Frank asking for an introduction to Ernest Bloch, with whom he was hoping to study music. Frank's reply commented positively on a letter of Toomer's that had been published in *The Call*—undoubtedly a welcome note of encouragement to Toomer, who had been writing steadily for two years and was anxious to see his work in print.

A year and a half passed before Toomer resumed his correspondence with Frank, and his 1922 letters laud the man he was courting as a mentor. Frank replied with the sort of complimentary affection that must have flattered the twenty-eight-year-old aspiring writer. "Glad I was to hear from you, and to read what you had to say," Frank wrote.

> You are the sort of life one doesn't forget . . . nor do you grow dim. . . . Yes: Washington must be a lonely place. . . . But I wonder if you are lonelier than I am here in New York? . . . We must still persevere alone . . . all of us, scattered suffering, fighting the pain and the menace of under-nutrition of which you speak. . . . Your letter has helped enormously. I wish I could think I could be of help to you. You are one of those men one must see but once to know that timbre

> and the truth of. About you at present solitude and silence. Well. mine is broken mostly by the bile-venting of ugly journalists who hate me with a hate I can never understand. And then letters such a [*sic*] yours, not changing my silence, but filling it with sweetness. (3 Apr. 1922, Toomer Papers)

Before a month had passed, Toomer sent Frank a batch of his writing—the sketches that would become *Cane*—and Frank responded positively and in generous detail. It was clear, he wrote, that Toomer had "a vision," but he asserted that "the Form is not yet there." He offered detailed suggestions for refining the texture of the writing—a significant critique, given that Toomer's lyric style is generally held to be his greatest strength. Frank concluded, "I am enormously impressed by the power and fullness and fineness of your Say. . . . A man whose spirit is like yours so high and straight a flame does not need to be told that he has enormous gift[s]" (25 Apr. 1922, Toomer Papers). The multipage response closes with "your friend and brother," an endearment Toomer seized for the opening of his next letter a week later. Thereafter, the two men addressed each other as "dear brother" or "brother mine," an explicit testament to their fondness for one another.

Frank made plans to visit Toomer in Washington during the spring of 1922, but he was prevented from doing so by the imminent birth of his son, Thomas. He planned another trip to the South—a research trip for *Holiday*—for the early fall of that year,[3] telling Toomer, he was looking for "some small town with a typical division of white and black folk" because he wanted to gather material for additional chapters—one on the Jew and one on the Negro—to add to *Our America*. "I am going to stay there ad [*sic*] just collect and refresh my thoughts and emotions, the maturity of two trips South these past years," he wrote. "Want to come with me? DO!" (17 July 1922, Toomer Papers). Toomer accepted the invitation with great enthusiasm and began describing possible locations. "What little I know is freely open to you," he insisted (25 July 1922, Toomer Papers). As their plans progressed, Frank explained his goals in greater detail:

> Here is my need, Jean, as regards town. My novel is to be called HOLIDAY. And it is simply the story of a lynching. The picture of the drab hideous unpainted town of the whites, the niggertown next-door, possibly in a marshy pinewood: and the gradual tunescence that ends in the Passion of the burning. A short, swift novel, all living in my head except the actual words. Now what I want, just incidentally, is to be once again[4] in such a town . . . where there are such white persons, and such black ones. Is Kentucky the place? is it sufficiently *south*? What about one of the Carolinas? They are not so far as Georgia, and are the precise thing. But I have no objection to Kentucky, or

Arkansas or whatnot. It is up to you, dear brother. Let us simply not squander money on railroad fare: not go any farther, that is, than is needed. You understand of course that what I want is not to photograph in my book the town we choose: I have that town clear already and it is not a factual town. But I wish to soak once more in the color and atmosphere that first inspired my idea. That is why I wish an ethnic similarity and an economic and cultural [one] as well to that first inspirer.

You are good to say what you do about the promise of HOLIDAY (dont tell the title to anyone). I am probably presumptuous to write about the Negro, and particularly since I know you who are creating a new phase of American literature (o there's no doubt of that my friend). Of course what my book will be is something far apart from your own: I see a dynamic form, a rather abstract Design of this juxtaposition of repression and passion. My book will after all be of its source . . . probably the most purely subjective Design I have ever created, precisely because of the extreme objectivity of its subject. (26 July 1922, Toomer Papers)

Toomer used his grandfather's name and family connections to arrange the trip under the guise of writing a volume on the African American race involving "social and biological science." His queries to Jesse E. Mooreland, the Howard University trustee and theologian whose collection of black American history helped establish the Mooreland-Spingarn Research

Center in 1914, gained him an introduction to President R. S. Wilkerson of State College in Orangeburg, South Carolina. Wilkerson suggested several towns the two might visit, including their eventual destination of Spartanburg, where they spent most of September 1922. Margaret Naumberg wrote to her husband in care of Mrs. Young at 398 South Liberty Street in Spartanburg; unfortunately, she destroyed his letters to her, leaving us to wonder what impressions of the trip he might have shared with her.

Frank was well aware of the unique advantages Toomer offered as a traveling companion in the South. "At whatever town we stay," Toomer wrote, "I'll have to be known as a Negro. First, because only by experiencing white pressure can the venture bear its fullest fruit for me. Second, because the color of my skin (it is nearly black from the sun) at the present time makes such a course a physical necessity. This, however, will not hinder our intercourse. Should make the exchange more complete, in fact" (15 Aug. 1922, Frank Papers). "Wherever we go, South, of course we go together," Frank replied. "If you go as a Negro, cant I also? What is a Negro? . . . so if you go as a Negro, so go I" (n.d., Toomer Papers). As Toomer and Frank both knew, the dark-complected Frank would surely be taken for a black man while traveling in the South in the company of a black man. Such statements should not be seen as an attempt by Frank to use Toomer's race to his own literary advantage, for, as readers will recall, Frank also commented, "I am probably presumptuous to write about the Negro, and particularly since I know you who are creating a new phase of American literature" (26 July 1922, Toomer Papers), to which Toomer quickly replied, "There is no poaching in the domain of pure art" (27 July 1922, Toomer Papers).

Following his return from Spartanburg, Frank struggled over his manuscript. "I've started Holiday," he wrote to Toomer, "but Spartanburg is not there at all. It's the gulf town milieu I spent so long ad [*sic*] painful weeks in, two years ago. Spartanburg gave me what I knew I needed: liberation: the possibility of writing about a negro without seeing and saying negro all the time. Anymore than when I write about a white man, I say white skin, white skin, all the time" (n.d., Toomer Papers). He completed a draft of *Holiday* by early November, as this entry in Notebook VIII attests: "Holiday in the rough is on paper," though it needed "hardening in places where the vision ran too loose" and "muscles" to "shape the words" (15). By March 13, 1923, the manuscript was in the publisher's hands.

Throughout this period Frank continued his correspondence with Toomer and offered to introduce his friend to various magazine editors. He also encouraged Horace Liveright to publish Toomer's *Cane*. In early January 1923 Liveright agreed, and Frank subsequently advised Toomer in intricate detail about the minutia of copyreading his page proofs, offering suggestions for dealing with copy editors. He wrote, "if there's any way I can help you get to NY I am ready." He also asked for Toomer's help in "reaching a possible Negro public for HOLIDAY," apologizing for the seemingly mercenary goal by explaining that the obligations of a wife and newborn (who was battling various illnesses) forced him to "think of sales" (n.d., Toomer Papers).

When Toomer finally made his way to New York in May 1923 to join the community of writers there, he was introduced to Frank's wife and the two quickly fell in love.[5] In early December 1923, while Frank was in Paris, his wife wrote to him with the news that she had decided to travel to Reno, Nevada, to obtain a divorce. Frank was probably unaware that Toomer traveled to Reno with Naumberg, having arranged for his elderly grandmother to misrepresent his whereabouts. Frank reacted to this personal crisis by focusing on his work. In February 1924 he wrote in Notebook VIII of his wife's decision to divorce him: "O sorrow, O frustration, O irony in this gap! But this is not a Diary: this is a *Work-Note-Book*. If you must *chatter* here, in lieu of putting down themes and creative ideas, at least *chatter* about work" (41). He then accounted for his work during the past year, noting that he had completed numerous writing projects (including fiction, reviews, essays, lectures, and a translation), had moved from Darien, Connecticut, to New York City and then sailed for Paris and Madrid. To be sure, his intense commitment to writing seems to have been a central tension in his marriage, even though the union itself was remarkably progressive and egalitarian. But his professional accomplishments offered little consolation for the failure of his marriage, and in the end Frank characterized the preceding months of acclaim—for *Holiday* included—as "Dismal lionizing and painful gaity" (Notebook VIII, 41).

Holiday was widely reviewed: some seventy notices appeared nationwide—a testament to Frank's stature in American letters—though some were less than laudatory. The *Cleveland Plain Dealer* announced, "Waldo Frank Gets Almost Intelligible" (19 Jan. 1923), while the *Greensboro News* noted, "Holiday Might Be a Good Novel If It Meant Anything at All" (11 Nov. 1923).[6] Much of the animosity seems to have been left over from reviews of Frank's two previous works, *Our America* and *City Block*,[7] and his reputation for elliptical prose and iconoclastic social critique surely biased some reviewers. But perhaps the most compelling feature of these reviews is the sheer range of highly passionate responses. Many reviewers balked at Frank's innovative style and used *Holiday* to berate literary modernism generally. The *Davenport Times*'s reviewer identified Frank's style as "modern to say the least. And to many it is the least." Henry Walker's review in the *New York Herald* had sexual overtones ("the usual ejaculatory series of verbal spasms which Mr. Frank strangely supposes to be English"), as did the review in the *Boston Herald*, which called the novel "jerky, spasmodic, and ejaculatory in style" but went on to say that "even Mr. Frank's absurd literary mannerisms cannot always conceal the vividness and poignancy of the picture."

As for the complex racial dynamic evoked within and around *Holiday*, one reviewer wrote in the *Portland Oregonian* that "Mr. Frank has had the fanatical courage to write a novel that is largely sympathetic to the negro's side of the case." This point was made more forcefully in the *Chicago Journal of Commerce:* "Mr. Frank presents the black people as they have seldom appeared in literature, with complete and sympathetic understanding. To the whites he is not so kind." But the most compelling reviews appeared in *Opportunity*, the journal of the National Urban League, and *The Crisis*, the literary arm of the N.A.A.C.P.[8] The review in *Opportunity* was written by Eunice Roberta Hunton (whose now widely reprinted essay "Breaking Through" first appeared in the *Survey Graphic* special edition mentioned earlier) and reveals her understanding of and respect for Frank's work:

> It isn't poetic prose. It is sheer poetry—poetry running riot, an epic too rich in beauty, hate, and tears to be

> held in the bonds of meter and form; now singing, now wailing itself to its tragic close through chapters painted clear by an author who has indeed probed America's open sore and dipped his pen in its blood, cleansed somewhat of its putridness by kind understanding. . . . And in the end one feels the author's hopelessness. He sees, he understands, and writes with piercing accuracy of the murk that rises from the swamps of the South—spreads over the land and is sucking it into its fetid depths.

Hunton's enthusiasm endorsed Frank's vision and his form, an appreciation that does not appear in Walter White's review in *The Crisis.* White, whose own lynching novel, *Fire in the Flint,* was published by Knopf in 1924, had narrowly escaped lynching himself as part of his work as an N.A.A.C.P. investigator in the South (though blond and blue-eyed, he was from a racially mixed background and chose to identify himself as a black man). His review of *Holiday* begins with praise, noting that "Waldo Frank has had the courage of the artist in treating such an episode and courageously handling it without sob-stuff, melodrama, or the desire to prove anything." But White, influenced by his own conservative literary style, also noted: "As it is, one is vaguely annoyed by the symbolic phrasing, the apparent irrelevancies."

Frank's perceived success or failure at achieving "racial authenticity" in *Holiday* became a matter of public discussion in the months after the book appeared. On September 9, 1923, he published a letter—"An Author to His Publisher"—in the *New York Herald*. The extensive commentary opens, "You tell me that certain reviewers of my new novel 'Holiday' have discussed it as if it were a tract on the negro problem, as if it advocated intermarriage between black and white, as if it had been written to air my views on a vexed question." After much hand-wringing, Frank reasserted his central vision, a Whitmanesque insistence on unity and truth: "To the artist there is no right and no wrong in this drama. There is only beauty, only truth, only life." His defensiveness no doubt resulted from long-standing battles with critics who relentlessly trivialized his work. A few weeks later, Toomer's review of *Holiday* appeared in *Dial* magazine and challenged the authenticity of Frank's depictions. Toomer argued that the characters were "essentially Frankian in origin" ("Waldo Frank's *Holiday*" 9) and that "whatever local or racial truth or untruth the work may contain must be considered as a purely secondary factor" (7). This is a strange critique, considering that Toomer reviewed the manuscript before it went to press and had written to Frank that "HOLIDAY is quite perfect as it stands" (n.d., Frank Papers).

The implications of Toomer's public charge were not lost on Frank and must have been a bitter pill for him to swallow, coming as they did from the man who had earlier written, "Nothing could have been more natural and real than our experience in Spartanburg. And the difficulties were extreme.... You not only understand CANE; you are *in* it, specifically here and there, mystically because of the spiritual bond there is between us" (n.d., Toomer Papers). Frank's private response to Toomer's published review of *Holiday* reveals his hurt and anger:

> Your opening paragraph *suggests* that in your opinion there is no meeting ground between my reality in Holiday and the reality which exists fundamentally in the South. I know you do not say this, and you do not believe it. But in your omission of the opposite, there is suggestion of this. And I regret it, because practically all the critics are jumping on me for not knowing the South, and you are the one man who knows I do, who was in a position to state so with some authority. (29 Sept. 1923, Toomer Papers)

Less than a week later he wrote, "Holiday is being slaughtered . . . among the 'influential' that simply astounds me. It's as if I am going backward, not forward" (1 Oct. 1923, Toomer Papers).

* * *

Rich in allegory and firmly grounded in the psychosocial history of the early twentieth-century South, *Holiday* depicts the simmering sexual and religious fervor that led to lynching. The novel is structured according to the cycle of a single day—dusk, dawn, noon, and dusk—that begins as a holiday from work for blacks because brutally hot weather has led their employer's daughter, Virginia Hade, to close down operations early at the request of John Cloud, the black overseer. The day is a holiday of sorts for whites too because the Revival Tent is being set up. Yet the religious passion aroused in the Christian men of Nazareth finds its final expression in the grotesque pyre they light beneath John Cloud, whose compelling figure elicits strong reactions, as revealed in the opening pages: "White folk . . . do not see how his height sings, they do not see how frail and hungry he is beside the pine. 'Big nigger' they see" (10).

The biblical metaphor suggested in the town's name is complicated by the arrival of the ship *Psyche* (during the docking of which a black sailor falls into the water and drowns because the white townsmen who can swim and might save him prefer not to get their clothes wet). Frank also presents readers with the evocative image of Virginia Hade and John Cloud being drawn together because they experience a similar restlessness, a sense of longing and unease described as a "skinny witch" that dances on the chest (165). Numerous biblical allusions suggest equally fascinating subtexts: John Cloud's initials indicate his role as a Christ figure as surely as Virginia Hade's given name announces her sexual purity; and the town's business of picking and preserving fruit evokes the Garden of Eden.

Frank writes in a rich and lyrical prose, yet he includes several provocative rhetorical tricks: for example, when the blacks in town address Virginia Hade in dialect, her surname sounds like "hate." By the novel's end, she sleeps quietly while John is horrifically killed, the implications of which are depicted clearly: "The *Psyche* stands at the empty pier that points from Nazareth out into the world." This is perhaps the most compelling image in the novel, whereby the author projects lynching in the broadest possible terms and painfully plots its psychological, social, and cultural dimensions. For readers who seek racial authenticity, *Holiday* may prove to be a disappointment; but for those who are interested in the psychological origins of mob action, who value an aesthetic democratic vision, and who believe in literature's power to convey the emotional logic of justice, *Holiday* will reveal itself as sobering, resonant, and memorable.

Notes

For permission to reprint previously published and unpublished materials I am grateful to the Waldo Frank Papers, Rare Book and Manuscript Library, University of Pennsylvania, and the Yale Collection of American Literature, Beinecke Rare Book and Manuscript Library, Yale University. A Faculty Research Grant from Oakland University financed my travel, and my work benefited from the helpful advice of Alyce DePree, Todd Estes, Bruce Zellers, and, at the University of Illinois Press, Theresa L. Sears. I deeply appreciate this assistance.

1. A well-respected magazine with a primarily white readership, the bimonthly *Survey Graphic* had previously ignored black American culture altogether. The special edition, which was edited by Alain Locke and became the basis of his important Harlem Renaissance anthology *The New Negro*, proved enormously popular, requiring two printings and establishing a record-breaking estimated readership of 42,000 (Watson 28). Note that *Holiday* appears in the bibliography of *The New Negro*, in the sections "The Negro in Literature" and "American Fiction since 1910."

2. Fauset's novel was reissued in 1989, and Toomer's exemplary collection is now recognized as a centerpiece of the African American literary canon and a hallmark of modernism.

3. Some scholars, including Paul J. Carter and Alan Trachtenberg, have mistakenly located the trip with Toomer much earlier, in 1920, but neither the correspondence between Frank and Toomer nor Frank's notebooks support this claim. See Carter (40) and Trachtenberg ("Chronology" xxxii).

4. On earlier trips to the American South, Frank traveled through Virginia, Louisiana, and Mississippi. In 1920 he gave a lecture on black music in relation to American music at the Tuskegee Institute in Alabama.

5. Toomer's biographers note that Frank initially "seemed to take Margaret and Jean's relationship in stride, but that became more and more difficult" (Kernan and Eldridge 113). Toomer's autobiographical sketches suggest that his friendship with Frank dissolved because he felt betrayed by the introduction to *Cane* that Frank wrote at Toomer's enthusiastic invitation, and he charged Frank with insensitivity to his (Toomer's) racially

nuanced identity (Turner 126). For many years, critics who were either ignorant of or chose to ignore the betrayal perpetrated by Toomer and Naumberg mistakenly accepted Toomer's account and branded Frank as racially obtuse. (For a particularly viotriolic attack on Frank, see Estes-Hicks.) But many of Toomer's letters to Frank contradict this claim. (For example, on receiving Frank's introduction, Toomer wrote: "I get a good feeling from the whole foreword. . . . Damn! what a job you had. Congratulations, and love, my brother. And THANKS!" [n.d., Toomer Papers].) A fuller discussion of the details of this complicated exchange can be found in Scruggs and VanDemarr (chaps. 4 and 5); see also Pfeiffer (chap. 4).

6. The reviewer for the *Greensboro News* went on to write: "No doubt the proper and conventional thing for a southern reviewer to do upon reading this book is to leap upon it with a wild yell of fury and accuse Waldo Frank of obscenity, lewdness, blasphemy, treason, murder, arson, rape, burglary, cheating at poker and probably harboring pro-German sentiments. As a matter of fact, however, none of these charges can be proved by 'Holiday.'"

7. Frank published *City Block* privately in 1922 because the New York Society for the Prevention of Vice threatened censorship over its alleged sexual impurity. The collection of sketches depicts the tensions, passions, and events of an urban neighborhood.

8. These two journals articulated the social and cultural aims of their organizations' founders—Charles S. Johnson, a sociologist, oversaw the National Urban League and W. E. B. Du Bois edited *The Crisis*—and were central to the promotion and dissemination of African American culture during the Harlem Renaissance and beyond.

Works Cited

Blake, Casey. "Waldo Frank." In *Dictionary of Literary Biography,* vol. 63: *Modern American Critics, 1920–1955.* Ed. Gregory S. Jay. Detroit: Gale Research, 1988. 122–30.

Carter, Paul J. *Waldo Frank.* New York: Twayne, 1967.

Davis, Thadious. "Race and Region." In *Columbia History of the American Novel.* Ed. Emory Elliott et al. New York: Columbia University Press, 1991. 407–36.

Douglas, Ann. *Terrible Honesty.* New York: Noonday Press, 1995.

Estes-Hicks, Onita. "Jean Toomer and the Politics of National Identity." *Contributions in Black Studies* 7 (1985–86): 22–44.

Frank, Waldo. "An Author to His Publisher." *New York Herald,* 9 September 1923.

———. *City Block.* Darien, Conn. Privately printed, 1922.

———. Correspondence with Jean Toomer. Jean Toomer Papers, Yale University, New Haven, Conn.

———. *Memoirs of Waldo Frank.* Ed. Alan Trachtenberg. Amherst: University of Massachusetts Press, 1973.

———. Notebooks VII–VIII. Waldo Frank Papers, University of Pennsylvania, Philadelphia.

———. *Our America.* New York: AMS Press, 1972.

———. Unpublished autobiography. Ts., Waldo Frank Papers, University of Pennsylvania, Philadelphia.

Fauset, Jessie Redmon. *There Is Confusion.* Boston: Northeastern University Press, 1989.

Hoffman, Frederick J. "Philistine and Puritan in the 1920s." *American Quarterly* 1.3 (Autumn 1949): 247–63.

Hughes, Langston. "Lynching Song." In *The Collected Poems of Langston Hughes.* Ed. Arnold Rampersad. New York: Vintage, 1994. 214.

Hunton, Eunice Roberta. Review of *Holiday,* by Waldo Frank. *Opportunity,* February 1924.

Hutchinson, George. *The Harlem Renaissance in Black and White.* Cambridge, Mass.: Belknap Press of Harvard University Press, 1995.

Johnson, James Weldon. *The Autobiography of an Ex-Colored Man.* New York: Penguin, 1990.

Kerman, Cynthia, and Richard Eldridge. *The Lives of Jean Toomer: A Hunger for Wholeness.* Baton Rouge: Louisiana State University Press, 1987.

Locke, Alain. *The New Negro.* New York: Albert and Charles Boni, 1925.

McKay, Claude. *Home to Harlem.* Boston: Northeastern University Press, 1987.

Ogorzaly, Michael A. *Waldo Frank: Prophet of Hispanic Regeneration.* Lewisburg, Pa.: Bucknell University Press, 1994.

Pfeiffer, Kathleen. *Race Passing and American Individualism.* Amherst: University of Massachusetts Press, 2003.

Review of *Holiday,* by Waldo Frank. *Boston Herald,* 25 August 1923.

Review of *Holiday,* by Waldo Frank. *Chicago Journal of Commerce,* 24 September 1923.

Review of *Holiday,* by Waldo Frank. *Davenport Times,* 18 August 1923.

Review of *Holiday,* by Waldo Frank. *Portland Oregonian,* 9 September 1923.

Scruggs, Charles, and Lee VanDemarr. *Jean Toomer and the Terrors of American History.* Philadelphia: University of Pennsylvania Press, 1998.

Stansell, Christine. *American Moderns.* New York: Metropolitan Books, 2000.

Toomer, Jean. *Cane.* New York: Boni and Liveright, 1923.

———. Correspondence with Waldo Frank. Jean Toomer Papers, Yale University, New Haven, Conn.

———. Correspondence with Waldo Frank. Waldo Frank Papers, University of Pennsylvania, Philadelphia.

———. "Waldo Frank's *Holiday.*" In *Jean Toomer: Selected Essays and Literary Criticism.* Ed. Robert B. Jones. Knoxville: University of Tennessee Press, 1996. 7–10.

Trachtenberg, Alan. "Chronology." In *Memoirs of Waldo Frank,* by Waldo Frank. Ed. Alan Trachtenberg. Amherst: University of Massachusetts Press, 1973. xxxi–xxxv.

———. "Preface." In *Memoirs of Waldo Frank,* ed. Trachtenberg. vii–xiv.

Turner, Darwin T. *The Wayward and the Seeking.* Washington, D.C.: Howard University Press, 1980.

Van Vechten, Carl. *Nigger Heaven.* Urbana: University of Illinois Press, 2000.

Walker, Henry. Review of *Holiday,* by Waldo Frank. *New York Herald,* 12 August 1923.

Watson, Steven. *The Harlem Renaissance.* New York: Pantheon, 1995.

White, Walter. Review of *Holiday,* by Waldo Frank. *The Crisis,* February 1924.

HOLIDAY

To my friend
Horace B. Liveright
in recognition of his great and many services
to the Good Cause of literature

Part One
DUSK

SUNSET at Nazareth.

Niggers go home through the copperglow of pines. Niggers sing home. White men stand lean in the doors of paintless houses. White men stand still.

The waters of the bay go red to the blue Gulf where swims the bloody sun . . sunset on Nazareth.

The Reverend Dill of the White Church cries:

"Air we gwine t' live up to our blessèd holy name? Air we gwine t' play cards 'n' dance 'n' drink co'n likker: or air we gwine t' be true t' the sperrit of our Lo'd Jesus Christ . . *hallelujah!* . . *he* nebber shot no craps, *he* nebber looked with lust upon no woman."

Nazareth. The Gulf of Mexico drains soil from her, blood red, to seas gray with moving. Moving seas of the world move athwart Nazareth standing . . *niggers move, niggers sing* . . a clot of crimson clay. But the trees sway up. And a dark man's eyes peer through the corridor of pine and yupon, he scents the flood of camphor leaves in the Fall:

—When the year dies why does she stir?
When the year dies why does she sing?

He is tall and slender. His height and slenderness is lithe. He is the color of dusk on the shadowed road he walks. White folk call him 'Lank.' They do not see how his height sings, they do not see how frail and hungry he is beside the pine. 'Big nigger' they see.

The road is behind him. Pines in this swampy world turn to cypress. Road in this lowering world turns to trail. The sky is a drum of drawn white skin: empty, beating emptiness. He walks. Voices rib under the white drum of the sky. Dark voices. Sorrow voices making hope. Song ribs the white sky whence the sun has fallen.

The ground is red . . sparse grass and needles spraying leave the ground naked: and the trees thrust up above their draping dimness into pale open. Sky is naked white, earth is red naked. Among the trees, between the sky and the earth, the dark begins to live.

It is inhabited by songs . . black flame . . that twist like horizontal rockets through the stanchioned silence.

Silence around the song. The cypress swamp a silence full of song.

"Ha-*o*. Ha-*o*. O watchin' skies ob de Lo'd."

A little skirt flicks white above black twirling legs. A little waist gleams white within black arms. Above the round head, hair thrusts like a pinwheel.

"How yo' feelin' John?"

"How yo' feelin' Mandy Smith?"

She is short: she prances straight to underneath his chin.

"I's *good,* when I's lookin' at you."

He smiles and touches the girl's hard cheeks that gleam in the dimness.

"Yo'-all late," he says.

"An' ef——?"

"Yo' Mammy, she'll be sayin': wha' yo'-all done in de dark?"

The girl's laughter, angular and strong, pierces up as her legs prance.

"An' I'll say to Mammy: 'Ah been wid Lank John Cloud.' An' Mammy, she'll stroke mah arm. She'll smile an' she'll say: 'O wid John? Well, dotter, da's alright. Ef yo'-all been wid *John.*' "

A scuffle of children's cries and bare feet beating brush lies yonder in the shadow.

Mandy skips away, her voice in laughter drawing a silver riband above the brown dance of her body.

A corps of children burst on him: stop.

"Done yo' seen her?" A boy with ripped pants and a hemp-hued shirt flared to his navel, all brown, all naked else, asks the question.

"Seen what?"

"Our goat."

"O yo'-all chasin' a goat?"

Three boys, four girls, hot, bronze with sweat, and the rags of skirt and pants laid casual upon their nakedness, stand and lift eyes on John.

"Yo'-all sho' she went this way?"

Seven black heads nod.

"Come along, then. Don't make such a racket, though. Steal up on her easy. She's suttingly hungry, jes' like yo'-all. She wants t' git home too. Yo'-all been too urgent: scar't her."

They fall in line with John. His arms point the fan form that their bodies docilely, instantly accept. They move into the trees. The song calls fill the silent falling night.

BENEATH a huge live oak is the cabin of John and his mother. Its weathered wood is mellow with the dusk that the great flood of leaves suffuses with green shimmer. It is symmetrical: its two rooms deep as the house, on either side of the hall that cuts through to the rear. A murmur of barn-life thrusts forever through to the wide open sward in front where tree-stumps stand, and a hitching post, and the chickens and the hogs by day lose their identity within the stillness.

Mrs. Cloud sits rocking on the porch, waiting her son. Odor of yam and cabbage and fried pork circles the quiet cabin, fends it off like a beneficent magic from the swamp's dank pressures. The live oak sleeps. Its streams of moss stand vertical within the gnarl of the wood. An early firefly studs the black of its low branches. The cabin hall is the cabin's throat. From the yard, through the cabin throat, come the thick stirs of animals asleep. A hog squeals wistfully. Yonder the bray of a mule sets momently on edge the firmamental stillness. . . John's striding feet punctuate the purple steadfast world like heavy bolts holding the wood of a chest.

He sees his mother waiting, rocking: he smiles.

"Sorry, Mammy. Meaghan's goat got lost. We had quite a chase."

"Come in, son. Supper's waitin.' Meetin' tonight."

She is serious and heavy. She gets up.

" . . 'n' Mary Cartier's comin' fo' to go 'long with us."

The cabin is propped above the clay. She steps down to the ground. Her son smiles at her serious way. He tucks his hands about her waist and turns her. There is the cabin above them: tall son smiling and a heavy woman nearer the ground, whose seeping dampness is heavy under the heavy garland of moss and of tree. But he smiles. And the cabin intercedes . . hands of a man musing, living, loving as he worked wrought this . . for the smile of John against the weight of his mother.

He bends so that his bronze cheek lies on hers. He helps her up, mock-painfully.

"Ol' woman—yo' gettin' lazy, yo' gettin' fat! Yo' cookin's too good. Mammy, soon I'll have to h'ist you."

Within the steam and cloy of the cooked food, she sits at his side. Her mood, with soil and tree and dying sky to strengthen it, pushes his smile away.

"John," she says, "I tol' yo' Mary Cartier's comin' fo' to go 'long with us. An' yo' sit 'n' say nothin', son."

"Ah heard you, Mammy."

"Ain't yo' glad, John?"
He looks at her, silent. —*It is your skin!*
"Ain't yo' glad, son, jest a bit?"

—Your love's a white sun shinin' on a sea.
Summer blue sea
Summer blue sky
. . Da's your love!
It is your skin!

"Why don't you answer yo' Mammy?"
"Mammy, fo'give me."
"Ain't yo' glad?"
"No . . No."
She shakes her head.
"I ain't sorry . . 'n' . . I ain't glad."
All that he sees is his mother: old brown hands, black at the nails, blue at the knuckles, clasp in wistfulness.

—Summer sea . . blue sky . . white sun . . *It is your skin!*

Her face is glowing with the youth of

her love. It turns away so that the lamp-light bathes it. Profile sheer with its high arched nose and its straight brow, with its thick mouth making a smile as delicate and fair as her handclasp.

—I love you, my mother. But it is your fault. You made me.

"Mammy," he says aloud, "I don't mind that Mary Cartier is comin' along to church."

"O you don't *mind.* Da's somethin'. Thanks." She studies him. "Yo' cares fo' her, son. Don' lie to me. Yo' does."

—An' I care fo' you. An' in my love fo' you, why is there blame?

"Dear Mammy," he says, "do yo' want so soon to get rid o' yo' son?"

She is stirred. She fights her feeling. She takes the last dishes from the table and carries them away. She faces the cupboard where they lie. She cannot escape the urgence of her mood. She returns to the table with its sooty lamp and the face of her son shining upon her.

"John," she says. And she sees not him, but the room where they are sitting. Sitting beside him, drawing the heavy chair to sit beside him, she sees the room that lives within her eyes . . their world she sees. A brown dark room, dark always, sun has never touched its crude-splashed plaster, the broad beams of the floor. Sun beats down upon the oak tree and its leaves turn sun into a green cool dance. Sun is a curse save the cool leaves transfuse it.

"John," she says: "John——" her hand moves toward him, draws his hand to the apron of her lap. "John, I fear."

He watches his hand held in the hand of his mother.

"Son, you are strong and good. Son, I am proud o' you. The cabin and the swamp, dey've stuck me here. But you are here, dey haven't took you from me. Not yet."

"Not yet?"

"Ah wants you always, John. Fo' I fear. I fear."

He understood. He lifted his hand a little to stroke hers.

"But Mammy, ef the cabin 'n' the swamp is *chokin'* me?"

"Chokin's our life." Her voice is harsh.

"It has been."

"An' it will be, John. O I knows I'm right to fear. Chokin' is de black man's life. Da's why he's black, I tell yo'. Choke a white man, he gits black too. Don' yo' dare dream otherwise. O John, I knows I'm right to fear!"

"Mammy, did I ever make to leave you?"

"It's de look in yo' eye. Ef dey ever fin' dat look, John, in yo' eye. Yo' done fo'get about yo' Uncle Wallace. My brother Wallace. He had a dream lak you. What was it? Nothin', John. Jes'—to stop chokin'. Jes' a dream of a black man's breathin' free. An' de dream gave a look to his eyes. An' wid his eyes he went to de White Town, an' he looked: looked at de sto's, looked at de cafés, looked at de men who called out 'Howdy, nigger.' John, John . . one day, wid dat look o' singin' freedom in his eyes, he looked at a white woman. He was lookin' at air: at free open sky; an' dat woman she got in de way of dat look in his eyes. An' somethin' in her eyes got kindled up by his. John, no mo'. Jes' de kindlin' look in his eyes and de kindled look in hers. John, no mo'. At nightfall, dey comes up. Right here. An' dey words was low: '*Git out. Git quick.* 'Fo' de sun comes back, *git away.*' An' Wallace went."

"He went No'th."

"We lost him, No'th."

A voice rose within the night. It clambered up, like a swift dark flying flower.

And when it reached the ranges of the night, it sang:

"Deep River. . . Deep River."

And when its song was done, it wafted down, a flower with wings falling, till it reached the clay of the night's red sleeping floor. And it slept.

"Mammy," said John, "how lovely is our world."

"We lost him No'th."

"Mammy love, don' you see? I'll never go No'th. Don' you see how I loves . . how I loves——" A faint breeze rising scudded in the cypress trees and turned a silver whisper wide in the black night.

"How I loves . . how I loves . . our land!"

"Ours," she swings her head in irony. "Our land!"

"Didn' yo' hear dat song? It was a woman of ours. Didn' it fit right perfect in de night? Don' the night lie homelike on our town . . ?"

"Niggertown."

"Yo' ought to see the night yonder on Main Street, Mammy. Night's all broke up with jagged ugly lights. Night's runnin' away from Main Street, all de time. It's our night, Mammy, an' it's our red lan'."

She has dropped the hand of her son.

"—an' it's our white sun."

Her face is full on him: her eyes confront his eyes that do not see her. Her face is sharp with a dawning horror.

"Son," she murmurs, "have dey already seen dat look o' yo' eyes?"

He laughs. He strides with his bolt-like steadfast march from corner to corner of the room.

"Our land! Our night, it is! Our breathin', singin' world!" His striding feet hammer the room shut. She is afraid of her son. His voice flames in the cabined room.

Room is shut and dark, the flame of his voice lances free. She is afraid for her son.

—Ah loves you, you is mine,
Sweet dark lan' o' de South:
Yo' eyes wi' deir swayin' shine,
De sweet song o' yo' mouth.
What are de niggers singin'?
Ain't it de breath o' de South?
You mine, O lan' o' de white snow
stalks over de red soil swingin',
You mine, fo' my song an' yo' song
Am de breath o' my mouth.

He has stopped as his moving will went upward into song. With the last words he stands erect in the corner of the room, and his head is high in the shadow of the rafters. His mother, short sheer bulk by the lamplight, watches the height of her son: watches the look of his eyes.

She moves to him. She sinks to her

knees. Her hands go up, like the flutter of old leaves. Her voice goes up, clearer, straight like the gaunt black trunk above the autumn leaves.

"Son," she says, "I fear. Jesus, be merciful to him who has de look dat's danger!"

He lifts her up: her brown face close to his, now stooping.

—*Your skin.*

"She's pretty, is Mary Cartier. She'll make you safe. She's smart. She'll wash away dat look. Marry her, son."

"When I marry——"

"You better. You twenty-three next April. A man needs his woman. Else his eyes go lookin', else his eyes go huntin' . . "

Knock. Mrs. Cloud rises, lightly for her, her hands already wide to greet Mary Cartier who steps in.

The lamplight makes of the girl's bare throat, bare arms, a luminous darkness. Her features, curved and full, stand out from the black wood of her hair as if some sculptor with chisel and knife of flame had fashioned her from earth. She smiles. A faint side toss of her head infuses a murmurous movement to her face that makes her presence in the heavy room a sort of song of the night.

She kisses the old woman. She gives her hand to John.

"How yo' feelin', Mary?"

She smiles, saying no word. He sees her teeth gleam white above the blue-hard gums.

"Ah'll be ready in a minute, dears. John, yo' keep Mary company till I tidy up." Mrs. Cloud disappears.

The girl and the young man feel the room suddenly harden its walls, sharpen its angles to contain them. He feels the rondures of her flesh, she feels the single pressure of this man and of their knowing each is there with each.

She goes to the armchair. Her way is musing. He stands stiff and clear.

"Mary," he says, "Mammy wants fo' us two to git married."

She seats herself, and then she looks at him. Her eyes smile wistful but her bared teeth take on a gleam harsh and savage as a crying voice.

"You don' want to marry me, John?"

"I sho' do love you, Mary."

"John, O I love you!"

"Ken I kiss you, hon'?"

She gets up for him. Their bodies move with gentleness upon each other, link in a fierce moment. She puts him off.

"I'm afraid of you, Mary."

"You love me, John?"

"I can't . . marry . . "

"Not yet."

"You understand?"

"I loves you, John. Go ahead. I want fo' to make you happy."

"Ef you understand, tell it to me——"

She laughs. "Ain't much to tell. Yo' ain't ready, da's all."

"Why, Mary?"

"Yo' too *alive* yet, I reckon, fo' marryin'. Only fo' marryin'." She holds out her hands.

"Mother's afraid." He clasps them. "So afraid, she wants you to take me now, while I'm so much alive. . ."

Her face loses its luminous warmth. It turns away to the wall, to the world beyond the wall. It is hard like coal.

"I hate them," she mutters. "All of 'em, I hate. Deir cold hot eyes dat look at you, wantin'—hatin'."

They stand this moment lost from sight and feeling of each other in a common cloud. (*White folks wanting, white folks shutting down, white world hungering and a cold hard hate, a hating poison from its hungering love.*) They have lost each other. Sudden they seek each other. Hand clasps feverishly hand and draws the burden of the other's fear . . warmed fear . . closer to it, closer.

"John," her voice is the call of that in her is voiceless. His arms about her drink the sweet comfort of her yielding body. And a rocking gentleness enarms them standing, within the cabin, within the white gaunt pall of the world.

Mrs. Cloud has a shawl about her head.

"Mammy," says John, holding the hand of Mary. "Mammy, I hope you won't mind *too* hard. Fo' Mary Cartier and me is thinkin' of gettin' married."

WHITE Nazareth longs across the bay to the City yonder. Nazareth cannot see the City, but it is always there. And when the daily steamboat carries you at dawn an hour from Nazareth, the City's towers stand white in haze: and about you is the green jetsam of the Gulf: and Nazareth has died behind on its clay bank fringed with pine.

White Nazareth thrusts down longing to the bay. Main Street narrows in resolution. The frame stores, tin fronted, lose their pride, lose half their being. The red street dips and all its will is bayward. The stores, crowded, are shoddier. The street is strident with cacophony of gutter, of twisting rut and groove. On the loose-beam bridge street leaps a gully, red through water oak and holly: street flares into a tongue of wide moist land which is the way to the pier. The longing of white Nazareth is the pier: Nazareth's longing for a towered world, a world of trolleys and department stores and liners from Honduras plethoric with fruit. The pier is very long. It is rickety, moldy, bulging. It is narrow, it is uneven, its railings are gapped. It is full of boards splintered, boards dangerous to step on, boards with nails gaping orange through a spray of rot. The pier is the cluttering broken wooden will of the town, thrust out . . half mile of water . . into the bay of the world.

Dusk. Nazareth trails down, trails out to meet the ***Psyche*** which for a score of years has dumped bags, barrels, weary feet upon a patched-up pier. Dusk. The town lies straggling on the rugose street, gray like the shell of some archaic bug whence the black blood has oozed. Nazareth living flows the reddish slope to the low waters. Each drop of the dark blood has a face pale and drab like the stiff houses stuck against the sky. The angle of their frames, the paintless beams, the false tin fronts find their mysterious counterpart in nose and eye and mouth of the white human stream.

Nazareth moving down is apart from the world, and it remains apart. Red earth, blue bay, whitening sky round to the monochrome of dusk. And within, flecking the world's rapt sweep, the houses like splinters, the faces like dry flakes, jagged thoughts, pressed passions. . .

Where the pier widens at the end, the stream of Nazareth widens and stands still. The bay, suntouched, is a saffron sheath. From it a tiny spot, dimensionless and colorless, sends a faint whistle: the whistle lingers and stings after it is gone. In the minds of waiting Nazareth, the *Psyche* grows: grows from the penetrant pierce of the whistle upon the silken bay . . now yellow, now suffused in rose . . until there is a boat, thrusting aside water, spitting, churning, groaning, soiled flat white: coming in full steam up.

Bells clang clang . . clang . . clang one two three. An odor of warm salt wafts with the steam and the wet wood and the hemp up the pier that seems to slide upon the steadfast steamer. She swings in sidewise. From her bridge, a man, cavernous eyed, casts angular remarks upon the deck, upon the crowd. Negroes, purple in dusk, move with ropes, cast them: the crowd stirs thickly as the ropes come scuffling. They are caught. They are taut. Steamer and pier move in upon each other over the gape of the water, like two adverse wills welded by will beyond them. A negro slips on the greasy, narrow deck. His legs stick up: with legs and arms thrust skyward, he strikes the water between the pier and the boat. The crowd rustles back, holds back as if the falling negro drew it down. A man at the bow casts a plank that holds the gap between the boat and the pier. The boat halts shivering, it stands resistant, as if the fallen negro drew it too. The water foams. Black boys peer wondering and aloof upon the frantic head. White men glance with guilty eyes away from each other. The black head sinks. Watching Nazareth is hushed before the word of the black head disappeared. . .

"Cast that there plank:" the strident skipper's voice. The gap of water, stilled, narrows away. Steamer and pier kiss slowly.

Once more the plank is thrown in its proper place. Wagons, barrows, crates, a shuffle of white faces, a strewing of black, move from the boat to the pier.

"Too bad. . . Who was it?"

"O, one of them Town niggers. Not ourn. They change ever' week."

"Why didn' one of his own go after him?"

"Huh! Them niggers? Catch 'em. Dey can't swim, nohow."

Virginia Hade comes through the press, comes up to a tall man whose eyes greet her with awareness of her words ere she speaks them.

"Hello, Sis," defensively.

"Bob: one of the boys go over? True?"

He nods.

"Why didn't you go after him, Bob?"

"Why should I, Virginia? Plenty o' niggers round. Why should *I?*"

"You swim well enough."

He pats the smooth thigh of his flannel trousers.

"Virginia, cut it. Here at least. It was one o' the niggers, I tell you. I didn't have time to think. Got sucked in between. It wasn't my affair."

The stream is flowing back to Nazareth.

"You wouldn't have thought so carefully, if it had been a White."

"Course I wouldn't. That'd been different, I reckon. Eh—wouldn't that have been different?"

"Yes," she says. And he is satisfied.

Young man, young woman, flow along with the stream. The sheath of the bay pales to a silver film over orange, over black. The sun is gone. Above gray pines, a moon at full stands pale. The red cliffs glow like copper.

THE trees of Niggertown hold night sternly.

Mary Cartier with John and Mrs. Cloud come down the steps of their cabin, going to Church. The trees hold the night. Night is held moveless and warm. Young man, old woman, girl move in the perfect night. The cabins make their fire-signs, sparse and scattered among trees, within night. The cabins are shadowed secrets thrusting into night swift words of lamp and kindling that are dream: for the cabins brood about their dream-hid flame, blacker, more somber. Flame of voices too. Mothers croon lullabies. Babies jet their savage lambent cries into the womb of silence. Boys shout cadences of play. Girls make calls over dishes, that paint soft throats. Through the manifold corridor of pine, of cypress, of yupon, holly, cedar, move the feet of the erect, churchward . . skyward.

—*Dere shall we meet!*

The church stands in an open patch of the woods. Tree walls lean back and the sky presses in. A clump of buggies casts lamp-glow on the unpainted loom of the long church. It stands fantastic, insecure among the trees, bathed in the pallor of the hidden moon, and the wagon-lamps gashing its flank. The threshold of the church is black and choked with a murmurous people. The open ground takes the sky thirstily. Cabins fronting it are dark. Their flames are dead, have left the cabins dead. A well in the center of the open space rises like a rock within the mist that swims upon the grass: and in the mist the stars.

MAIN STREET fights night. Jaggedly brittle, along the rugose road, Main Street fights night. Electric lamps, displays of drugstore, movie, specialty shop, the angular thrusts and jerks of house fronts . . cut the night like an ugly blade: drive night far off and in the road lie fragments of its deep . . shadows . . like shards.

The dwellers of white Nazareth fight night. Young men stand in the storeways. They are lean and motionless. Their heads upon their necks do not turn. Their faces do not speak. Their words are ejaculations of a static sense. Thought and sentiment and passion dwell fixed within a moveless pivot of their souls. Others not lean, not pallid. That which is moveless within bursts out: big fellows with flourishing mustaches, bushy brows. They are obscene with brutal energy that bursts forever out in their gruff ways, their obtuse thoughts, the raw of their voices.

Women, shut in night, fight the freeing night that lies spiked on white Nazareth. Women pale and wistful. Their languid mouths move half against the hunger of their eyes and the denied mist-longing of their hair. Fair skins, transparent like December's moon at sunset. Sky of the sun, sky of the crimson soil sicklies the broken turmoil of their youth.

But the night flames up. Moon mounting floods the pine woods. Stars fade gold against the washing softness of the moon. Stars dance, stars swing. The sky is a blue song, worded with golden stars. The sky is a blue scarf jeweled with starlight, flung about the moon. . . White Nazareth sits upon her damp red clay and spikes her shanties into the heart of the night.

Virginia Hade walks to her church on Main Street.

(In the swamp a cypress tree, above the breathing of the nearer pines, sings aloud:

—Where is the golden dust that made
me thirst?
Night is a tide of silver. Day is a
drouth of gold.

The tree frogs jangle:

—The land swims and the water
wants to walk.

The nigger church out yonder in the swamp stands mightily with arms upthrust: it trembles, it swerves, it drowns the murmur of pines: it leaps above the trees:

Ha' Mercy, Lo'd! . . .)

Virginia Hade walks between nods on Main Street.

Stiff boys bend, slack women stiffen, big-browed men grow sharp of eye and querulous of heart as the straight girl walks. . . (A nigger head bobs in the water. Screams. White laughter presses the black head down into a dirty bubble.)

—We look up to you, Miss Virginia. We-all are proud, right proud of you, Miss Hade. God bless you. Your going to church does us a heap o' good. God bless you, Miss Virginia.

—I believe. And Christ and all the Apostles, they were like us. *Were they like us?* O yes: they were like us. *Were they?* The writers of the Book, the speakers of the Word . . all—*were they?*—like us?

The new white church is a blaze of light. Revival Week. A printed banner is strung between the church and the opposite portico of a stable:

COME AND BE SAVED

IF JESUS DON'T GET YOU

THEN SURE SATAN WILL!!

Muffled men and women move from the night into the electric smile of the church whose door gapes like a mouth.

" . . . *Let us pray* . . ."

With shuffle, rustle, the worshipers bow their heads. Eyes behind fingers, faces peering upon laps and trousers, brows horizontal over sweated shoes . . seek God.

Virginia Hade is late. She walks down the aisle. The grace of her strong way is broken by a strain vising her hips and her dark eyes that meet the gleam of the candelabra. She is tall and firm, but her harmony is broken and her eyes are not happy. She sinks in the dry human sea. Her black eyes fade in the welter of many bodies: her golden hair stands out.

The Reverend Dill is a sleek form holding a face contorted in supplication. His palms press high above his working face: and his mouth twists as he wrings from it God's words.

Dry rustling sea of women, girls and men.

" . . We pray you, Lord, give us a sinner, just one more sinner, tonight. For Jesus' sake. . . . "

There are no waves on this sea. The preacher's voice is acid shrill . . no waves . . his hands swing sharp . . no waves . . hate and accusal lance from his wrung mouth. The dry sea lies before his frenzy, chill in his chill heat . . no waves, no waves.

" . . O Jesus Christ. . . "

This sea is flat. If it has waves, they sleep below. They pray for the preacher to have whipping words to lash the surface, to make it roar and foam.

—We are rolling underneath
 Secret waves.
 O we want the stars, O we want the
 sun

Secret waves.
Cannot the free winds whip us?
We crowd within: *God let us out!*
Come, preacher, lash us! Make us
leap!

The sleek preaching figure prances to and fro. Where is the ancient virtue of fear? the magic of exhortation? . . Dry flat sea.

Eyes of men wander with gelatinous leisure: eyes of women draw in, knowing the eyes of men. Discomfort sits heavy underneath the electric thrust of the preacher, the electric blare of the lights. His words shrill. His hands open and shut. He shoots his words like a creature at bay from a recess of fear within him. "God" shot with fear. "Christ" cast with venom. "Hell"——with gloating. God, Christ, Hell conjoin in a beating wind . . outside, outside, beating against this waveless stifled sea.

Splendor all about the worshiping church. The world is splendor. The church is an atom, coruscant and hard, against a living splendor.

"AN' Saul . . da's Paul, brethren, da's Paul . . yet breathin' out threatenin's an' slaughter ag'in' de *de*sciples o' de Lo'd . . Amen, Hallelujah . . he went unto de High Priest,

"An' desired ob him letters fo' Damascus . . dat ef he foun' any ob dis way . . any ob de Christian way, folks, does yo' hear? . . whether dey was men or whether dey was women, he might fotch 'em back bound to Jerusal*em*.

"An' as he journeyed, brothers, an' as he journeyed, sisters, an' as he journeyed near Damascus on—— *O* sudden there shined round him a Great Light fum Hebben——"

"Amen." "Hebben." "Mercy, Lo'd!"

"An' he heard . . Paul did . . a Voice a-sayin' to him: 'Saul, Saul, why persecutest thou Me?'"

The black man was upon his knees. His great rich voice beginning in a sob . . "Saul, Saul" . . rose sharply with the "why," rounded the hard syllables of the next long word, rose, fell: and his hands, clenched near his brow, shook in the strain of his passion.

The black church hushed. The dim lamps thrust their silent hands along the rustic walls. The ceiling was hidden. Black, it moved up there with the deep waves of prayer. And the crude pews broke with their thick multitude, black, also, also hidden.

The preacher sprang to his feet, his clenched fists spread into enormous hands. His mouth was wide: "O you——" The worshipers, locked in the Pity of Christ, broke now in his Glory. Hidden still in the commanding gloom, their voices rose, a burning and a jungle:

"Ha' mercy, Lo'd."

"Good Paul."

"Good Jesus."

"Hear."

"Amen, amen."

"Ha' mercy, preacher."

"Christ."

"So he did."

"Da's right, preacher. Da's right." . . .

"O you," cried the black prophet. His round thick body was erect. Sweat flowed from his bull head and his neck. His broadcloth suit wrinkled as his muscles worked. He prayed:

"O you, does you hear? O you, does you hear de Lo'd? He's a sayin': Brother, Brother. He's a sayin': Sister, Sister." Feet beat time. "How long yo'-all gwine fo' to cheat me?" Feet beating time lifted his voice to song. "How long yo'-all gwine fo' to leave me out in de col'?" . . "Nevah! Come in! Lo'd take me!" . . "Why do yo'-all persecute me so?"

The preacher was on his knees again, voice high.

"Does you see Him up dere? Folks, hear me. Does you see Him up dere? Folks, hear me. Down dere . . don' you see down dere de Devil?"

Feet beat. "Ha' mercy." "Da's right." "I sees him."

"Which will it be?"

Silence. The preacher uprose. His arms shot out and his voice:

"Which will it be? Christ's beggin'. Christ, he ain't proud. Christ, *he* ain't like yo'-all niggers. He done got spat on. He turned de other cheek. Dey lynched him, Christ. He prayed fo' 'em. He come back: sayin': Saul, Saul, I loves you yet. He ain't proud, Church. Does you hear me? He's a-callin' you. An' so's de Devil."

"Ha' mercy, Lo'd."

"Church, you gotta choose!

"Church, you gotta *se*-lect!

"Church, which shall it be?"

He moved to the platform's edge. He crossed. He re-crossed.

"Paul's a-walkin' de Damascus road. A-threatenin' blood and slaughter. Does yo' see him, Church?"

He walked, he walked. He was Paul. His voice was a strange song weaving his way on the Damascus road; and the immanence of mystery in his eye and the full hate behind him. The vaulting, beating breath of the hid multitude was the world about his way.

"He's a sinner. Like us. A-walkin' to Damascus. When he sets eyes on a Christian, Paul's eyes flash hate; Paul's hands dey strike de Christian. An' he's a walking de Damascus road, sent by de Devil. Proud! Stuck-up! His clothes is rich. He's got pull, alright, he Paul. He votes. He's a real white man, a-struttin', full o' hate."

The preacher strutted, back and forth.

His hands were tipped in the armpits of his vest. No words . . a rocking croon came now from his lips. And the worshipers beat along, foot beating, body swaying: lambencies of cry and word shooting through the livid night of the church.

"O—— *OO!*"

The strutting prophet crumpled. The worshipers' beat rose fierce like a wave upon him. All is still.

From the moveless body on the floor:

"Wha's dat light? What am dat blindin' fire? Ah can't see. . ."

"Jesus——Jesus."

"Fire ob Hebben. Ah'm all knocked down. Mah eyes is full of fire an' of smoke."

"Jesus——Jesus."

"It's de Lo'd! Dah he is. Dah in de darkness, he's de fire!"

"Jesus——Jesus."

"Mah head's in de dust. Mah eyes am full of blackness and of dust. Ah'm down,

Lo'd. Ah been a struttin' high and crool. Ah'm down, Lo'd."

"*Ha' mercy!*"

"Ah believes."

The black head thrusts up. His crumpled body comes to life.

"*Jesus——Jesus.*" Beat . . beat . . beat.

"Ah been a sinner, Lo'd. O—O what a sinner!

"Ah been a sinner, Lo'd. O—O lemme up!

"Ah been a sinner, Lamb. O—O lemme belong!"

The prostrate man rises in dignity. He stands silent above the quaking church. No singing voice, a monotone as sharp as a steel rod moves from his mouth.

"Church: da's what Christ done fo' Paul. Da's what Christ is a beggin' fo' to do fo' you."

The church trembled as if the sudden prose of the singing preacher had prodded it awake. Slumbrous before and agonized in darkness whence came broken words, fragments of prayer, now as one it rolled up into song. The worshipers sang. Their bodies swayed, eyes gleamed in the hot dark. Song swelled the church, billowed the rafters and the walls; the whole church was a throat pouring its music forth upon the night.

The preacher prayed. He was bowed and exhausted. With his sweat-soaked handkerchief he mopped his brow, his eyes, his hands, his neck. He prayed, while the cloth went mopping: with shut eyes, faintly asway in the song-storm of the church.

And still the song grew thick. The church was a cauldron full of a thick song brew: rising, thickening, boiling, as God stirred. The church fell away, burned up its wooden walls and rafters: it was Voice. . .

Stillness at last. The church was a dark silence more alive than song. It was a cavern of dark life. The preacher stood in awe above its deeps: held by a pregnancy.

Single voices of a man, of a woman from the new dark womb: tonguing up, falling back into the aching pentness. . . A girl rose clear. Her head and her arms spiked out into the lampglow. Angular arms thrust, legs beat a dull reiterant tattoo . . stiff, catatonic . . while her head lurched forth, lurched back, lurched sidewise and her arms spun like the arms of a mad marionnette.

"O Lo'd. . . O Jesus. . . Mercy on me, Lo'd."

Her voice, her arms, her head, her rigid legs held back the ecstasy of the crowd, held up her splintering frenzy. From her brown dress it came: body gleaming black, prayer burning black: body and prayer came one. She danced. Her feet struck the floor. Her arms pierced the round chant of the church. She danced. She was a sharp fierce dancing gem in a world murmuring round her like a moving matrix. She crumpled. She fell to silence.

Song rolled released. It was steadfast now, unmoving from the house for the house and the world moved with it. Song conquered. It was almost quiet song. Chants, shouted prayers, swift confessions in the luminous shadows as men and women rose, danced, sank away . . lived within the song like blood within a moving body.

MIDNIGHT.

The nigger church has let out its dark flame substance. It stands a shell under the moon. Mist is gone from the open. The trees crowd close, they are pressed by the high moon into thick comradeship, the moon falls on their heads and is repelled. Stirred souls have wended off, carrying through the corridors of night where the sky's blare is hushed a luminous music. Myriad ways music has flowed forth from the emptied church, filling the woods; from the pale church lighting the woods. Music dwells in the beds of crude cabins, under shut eyelids, weaving breath and heartbeat.

John Cloud is in his cot. He has walked with Mary home under the trees. He has not touched her hand. Perplexity spreads dominant through his will and wins him from her. He sees her face that glows in the darkness like a magical wood. He feels the warm of her body moving at his side through the questioning of trees, through the deep glances of trees. She says no word: —He has kissed me: He says no word: —Why don' I kiss her again? His mother's face stands close. —You are dark. You are dull. You do not glow like Mary's! Glow dies from faces that go on, go on. . .

Mary is home.

"John, thank you. Good night, John."

He takes her hand: in his hand it is burden. The trees are a black question. The cabin, that is her home, about a single lamp is a black question. The lamp will go out. The moon will go out. He drops her hand.

"Mary, good night."

And as he moves away a soft flesh tears. His moving from her through the dark, his carrying away with him the dark that lives beyond the glowing of her face, is sweet flesh tearing. Flesh joins this girl to him: —I must go. —When the lamp goes out, and the moon, and your golden face, when the dark is here, where is the light? *Out yonder?* . . His walking away lengthens and deepens the wound of Mary's flesh and his.

John Cloud lies in his cot. —*My flesh is whole!*

His cot is on the porch. Summer and winter, he sleeps with the damp night. Hot thunder rolls from the Gulf, white cold pours down the funnel of the Mississippi: his body, resting, takes them. Sleep is a sure peace whose balm lies swiftly near and casts its magic even upon the day. John is awake . . but easeful in his waking. Sleep is near.

In his shut eyes, as in the cypress swamp, stand the cabins of his folk. Crude logs, thatch, clay chime into grace. Here's mystery for here's beauty. John feels the alchemy whereby this pent black world, drenching in ignorance and pain and soil, shines fair. What is the magic?

But he longs away.

His body lies prone and sweetly wakeful within the magic of his folk. Yet part of him is uncovered, longs beyond: no glowing blanket of his folk can touch it.

—Away from the warm swamp with your
    cabin flowers
  Mammy, how wise you are!
Away from Mary with your warm bud
    breasts
An' your lips breathin' warm
I am cold.
  Mammy, how wise you are!
Can't you cover me?
Mammy, you grow cold too:
An' your skin is damp earth.
Nothin' that's warm can cover up my
    coldness.

Cold white world—I'll make you warm
—that'll warm me!

—There's a white dream stands between
my mouth and Mary's,
A white sunbeam in my soul.
I'll climb it. Tha's what it's fo'! I'll
vault with the white sunbeam!
Empty pale world . . world of the
Free,
Wait till I come an' warm you: wait
till I come an' fill you.

—Mary, the world is proud: world's a
white far-away woman,
But she's waitin' fo' me to pour my
flame inside her.
That ain't hate, Mary: she is waitin'
fo' me!
O Mammy, you're wise!
O Mammy, how little wisdom helps
when you're cold.

The afterglow of the calls and laughters of his folk sleeps in the night. Women's voices, uttering sorrow, sing. Men roll, men's eyes dance, lusting for a woman. Children's play is spirals of flame above the smoky earth.

Night is not made for thought. Fantasy dances in the oblique moon-motes. Vision tides like a sea upon the treetops, drenching the darkness with magic. John is asleep.

VIRGINIA HADE lies in her broad mahogany bed, awake.

—I am afraid of sleep. That's why my eyelids tremble and burn; that's why my hands hold rigid on my brow.

Thrust out your arms. That's right. Lie all stretched out.

There is a poison in your body, and it lurks in knots.

If you draw in your leg, the poison lingers.

If you cradle your face upon your elbow, so . .

Your lips close to your breast . .

The poison lingers.

Stretch out clear like a rod. Then you'll be clean.

O I want to go to sleep, I am weary.
O I want to wake up.

—Work is hard in autumn. The fruit is
pouring.
Orange, loquat, cumquat and satsuma:
The pecan nuts will fall in a shrill flood.
Ripe is their fruit, the trees go to sleep
in dulness:
Sweet dull winter of the trees when
they have given their fruit and the
leaves turn crisp and gray . .
some fall away.
God takes care of you, trees;
Yet you don't go to church, like I do,
trees.
Is it wrong to work?
How hard I work. . . Bob is a loafer,
and Papa's a Judge.
(*Smile at that.*)
How hard I work! And all my work,
. . orange, loquat, cumquat and sat-
suma . .

Ticketing
Answering mail
Billing and crediting and shipping
Sending the sugared fruit to the sour
North . .
What does it do but wear away
The shell of sleep
The shell of ease,
Baring the nerves that hunger?
Tiring my mind, tiring my decency,
So that my soul lies naked under this
black night!

—Yes, you are black:
Night, you're a raping nigger!
And the autumn day
with its golden sun
and its copperglow of leaf
and its red earth
I suppose you think you're white?

—I am a white soul naked
worn away and weary

Under the flood of color
Washed in the color sea
That is world, that is life!

—Lord, won't You let me sleep?
Look: I'm stretched out.
The poison can flow away, if only
You'll let it.
Sleep without dream . .
Tomorrow is work again.

—Sleep . . dream world . .
God, that's a Nigger too!
Color! Color! Color!
Everywhere.
Perhaps death is white?

—Sleep . .
dream world . .
writhing shapes writhe out
And stand upon my breasts
And stand upon my mouth
Forcing my lips!

I am all dark inside:
The world is dark flame,
Morn and noon and night
Dark dancing flame . .
I am all dark inside:
Perhaps death is white?

—They let a nigger drown.
Bob slapped his flannel thigh and let
a nigger drown.
Well, there are more of them:
More . . more . . more . . more.

—The night breeds 'em
And the boiling copper sun
Breeds niggers!
The shadows sun lays are dark:
And the earth, loam and clay, don't it
breed niggers too?

—Let a nigger drown.
God breeds 'em.

—And yourself,
You, Bob, with your huntin' lusts,
Don't you breed niggers?

—Why can't I sleep?
Are my insides dark?
Will they flood out if I sleep,
Wash my white soul black?

—Perhaps death's white . .
Perhaps my soul that's white
Is sister to my death!

—O I'm unhappy. That's why I can't sleep.
O I thresh about all day in straw
. . dry, dry . .
O I wrestle nights against dark forms of my soul
Breaking upon the dry white of my breast
Saying No . . saying No.

—My soul's not white!
Death's white: my soul wants to live.
It cries to live,
It sings to live,
It stirs within me like an unborn babe,
bleeding to live, all bloody with my blood . .
And my white breast says No.

—Why does the world say No?
Why don't I dare to learn how to say Yes?

—Soul, you're a little black babe under my heart.
Yes you are! . . I say it . .
Black as night
red as earth
golden as the sun,
my soul. . . . .

Then she slept.

Part Two

DAWN

THE dawn broke Nazareth into myriad things. Each thing stirred with sun.

Within the heights that fall in pinegroves to the bay, lie undulous red acres. Cotton sparkles white on black stalks ribbing the earth. Rectilinear orchards spurt in awry of orange, yellow, ochre. A cloud brightens above a haze of nut trees; the new wind finds dainty castanets for its dance. The earth swings from the bay, rolls, sinks to Niggertown. There the night lies longest, like a dankness sinking from the sharp thrusts of sun. The trees are thick; they huddle heavily like indolent invalids loth to arise from bed. A slumber, sealed by the dark branchbars, clasps the black town. But day has stolen in. While the night clamps its armor outwardly with trees, the barnyards are stridulous with dawn. Clamors of cock and hen are sparkles of sun: dogs howl low sun-rays: babies open eyes to hunger and toothless gums shriek thirst: aged women soak in the stir of dawn: old white-wooled men, listless with the torment of existence that has drained in with day and drenched their unresilient bodies, take wakefulness as purulent logs take water. Pumps creak, dishes jounce, a succulent glow rises from stoves. . .

John sleeps. His mother cuts slices from the new cured ham. John sleeps. The ham grows rich in the pan, sweating its savor. John sleeps.

She stands above his cot. And her eyes wake him.

"Well, son—well, son——"

He sees her through the waving of his sleep. His body, swathed in warm, lies sweet and takes in with wide eyes her and the sun's tip on the cornice of the porch.

His body takes in a world, all brightening, and the tang of the cooking meat and the accolade of cock and the tree's stir.

His mother's eyes hold a joy: her thought of Mary Cartier. She brings that pain to him with her joyful eyes. White Nazareth looms through the transparent trees: a poison he drinks daily. Dawn itsclf, virgin and ignorant, leads to day that is a well of poison.

John is up.

Nazareth's dawning sharpens, hardens. The dim hour was sweetest. Each soul lay restful in itself, came forth like a wild animal for nurture: each soul was nameless. Now Nazareth stands named! Nazareth matures. But while the sun moves up and the sky yields to its cruel naming clearness, dawn lingers where John eats.

The kitchen is hot and moist with night. The crude plaster walls are the color of dusk. A glow from the stove lies like a twilight sun upon the mother and man moving disparately upon one axis. Day is unreal here.

"Son," she says, "I slep' well las' night —thinkin' of you an' Mary."

"Mother, don' say nothin'!"

"Why, son?"

"Mammy, ever' mo'nin' I must get up and walk two miles to work. An' when I get to de Nazareth Fruit and Preserving Company, mah legs are tired. An' then I mus' work mah arms . . and mah legs too, Mammy. An' mah head, I got to fill it wi' thoughts of discipline: o' keeping de twenty dark folks under me happy an' in order. How yo' think I can answer yo' 'Why?' When I sleeps I sleep. An' when I wakes, I work. . . "

"Son, yo'-all had yo' fust quarrel quick as dat!"

"No quarrel, Mammy."

"You walked Mary Cartier home."

"Yes, Mammy."

"Dah was a moon, too. An' de preacher was movin'. God help us, son, ain't dat enough fo' lovers?"

"Mammy, we walked home, and we didn't say a word . . an' we didn't touch."

She laid her hands on her bulging hips, swaying perplexity, silent.

"I'll do what I said . . ef I can . . ef Mary keeps on bein' willin' to have me. Jes' what yo' dream fo', Mammy. But don' say nothin'."

He got up and reached for his cap. Mrs. Cloud was silent.

"Ain't dere voices enough . . ? In de woods, in de houses, in de sky at night? Ain't dere voices enough . . ?"

JOHN walks to work in the morning.

—Yonder my feet move me . . upon
true Nazareth.
Why are you dim?
This is the sink, the black heart and
the sink?
Why are *you* dim?
A flaming heart breaks, breaks in a
pale body.
Why are you dim?
You cast spells, Nazareth, you rule
. . . Dim!

. . The church is gaunt and has lost its voice and its life. Women at the well wield mellow bodies drawing water in the church-dry gloom. The path starts: autumn flowers are the wistful reaching of the broken earth toward sky unbroken. Mary's cabin stands at the wood's fringe: an iron grille shuts off a white farm whose pecans and oranges and honey are not for niggers. Mary bakes bread in the round clay open oven. She is clad in a frock earth-colored and her legs are bare. John stops and sees her head against the iron grille.—I loves her more at night. She walks demurely forward. He holds her hand.

"Good mo'nin', Mary."

"Good mo'nin', John." . . .

White world: the path's a road. Rail fences, telegraph posts, imported Duroc hogs red as the clay they snout . . a mile of farm and orchard disdaining Nazareth. Lean pines cupped for the turpentine, tall bloodless trees rising like white folk from the cloudy earth . . a gully dry and lush, spanned by an iron bridge (niggers built it and twenty white men have their names on the plate) . . white Nazareth.

The road's broad red. It rises till it strikes the fleckless sky: dipping, the town.

John is at the road's highest flare, held in suspense by the moving masses that lie about, thrust up to his steadfast point. The bay moves somnambulant to the Gulf that he can see folding the earth. On the escarpment the town lies splintering, a drab continuity from the pier to where John stands. Over his head, the sky. The man world wings to either side: it is lost in forest green and the roads, red bands, die dimming through checker cotton fields.

Darkest is Niggertown and murmurous.

He has walked through it in a haze of his mind that made him unaware. Now, the day's air . . water-swept and clean . . brushes to the brow of the earth where he stands, brushes the haze from his brow. —Mary and mother: your skin and the dim white Rule! He hears the murmurs of his world, now he has passed beyond.

—De Lo'd came down like unto Paul
    on de dusty Syrian Road.
De Lo'd came down an' dere was
    Mercy in His Han'!
De Lo'd came down an' His angry
    feet strode
T'rough de Heathen Lan' . .
Mercy in His Han'
OOOO yes
Mercy in His Han' . .
But His feet dey trampled—till dey
    bled
An' His feet dey trampled—till dey
    dead
All de doubtin' Heathen Ban'.

Murmur . . murmur of black Nazareth.

—Dey let a nigger drown! Dey smile an' say: Shall I wet my white trousers jes' 'cause a nigger'd drown? Big Bob Hade —he ken swim—fo' a prize. Slim Jim Cote—he ken swim—fo' any ol' white.

Dey let a nigger drown! Cl'ar befo' dey eyes. Dey let a nigger drown! Dat ain't right?

. . 'n' den . . 'n' den

Las' night in de Church
De Lo'd came down!

Black Nazareth, murmurous, rocks.

In the clear morn world the waters of the bay sleep still: and the orange cliffs are steadfast in the slowly mounting sun: and the white town stands: . . *black world rocking, black world beginning to rock . .* —You're a young girl's got love. *OO I loves you, Honey, OO I needs you.* You're a woman's lost her babe. *OO I needs you, OO I loves you.* You're a cloudy old witch has got religion. *Up yo' arms, out yo' arms. . . Yo' head throws black flame.* You, sideways in your swamp: Black Town . . what yo' murmuring for?

John Cloud looked forward. His heart

beat fast. —I fear. He looked forward down on the white Main Street. —Let me lean on you. You who rule. You who are civilized and white. Let me——why are you dim? when I need to lean on you?

The road was not dim. A lumber yard sprawled filthy. Logs, timber lay in clutter before the unpainted shed. The engine was within, grimed and obscene, thrusting its stack through the half-tumbled roof.

Lafe Tilson comes up. His huge hands red-haired run the sawmill: his huge mouth bawls orders to the niggers feeding wood. From the bushy brow, harsh pale eyes look out at John.

"How yo' feelin', Lank?"

"How yo' feelin', Mr. Tilson?"

The man scratched his ear.

"Mah niggers ain't come yit. Not so prompt, like yo'-all."

"Too bad, sah."

He sees John pass and irritation spurts

from his eyes. He loves to linger: engines and niggers for work: John has not lingered.

"Shed a been at the pier, las' evenin', Lank. Yo'-all swim."

He has sneered. John does not turn, striding a little faster into the hard white town. Tilson curses and spits.

"Damn his pride," he mutters. "Can't joke with a nigger. Treat 'em like a pusson—see what comes."

The schoolhouse, upon a lawn, stood away from the red road. Grass, gray, unkempt, lay about the pallid house like a rebuke. A chill rigor came from the shut windows: only a flagpole gleamed, catching the sun. A boy hoisted the colors: his scrawny arms seemed stiffened rope, as the striped cloth upfluttered.

John walks into the town. Before the drugstore . . where he may buy medicines, not *cocacola* (that is too near the social and calls for lingering and talk) . . cluster the town braves. The house about the drugstore is paintless like the others. It stands on piles; a porch is shedding wood, a false tin cornice holds the painted blazon. But in the windows are imported fineries of color and of shape: soaps, display ads showing pretty girls, garish candy boxes . . a strange invasion mocking the dull store.

Ten eyes see John. John sees Bob Hade, brother and son of his employers, and the town's champion swimmer (because he couldn't race a black).

—He was there on the pier!

An instant and John veils his look: an instant too late: John's look is out in the white world, five white men's eyes have caught it.

Hade tosses up his head. "Stop," he means.

"Well, Cloud?"

"How yo' feelin', Mr. Hade?"

"You're lookin' troubled, Cloud, this

mo'nin'. Kind o' pale . . kind o' pale, *for you.*"

Four men hunch perceptibly close, sustaining their leader.

"Ah don' know what you mean." John's body is held stiff against the tremble of his hands, the gathering rage of his eyes. If he moved . . he wants to move . . it would not be away!

Hade snickers.

"Hope you'll be feelin' better, Lank." He has had the release of his insult: he is kindly again: he is the tolerant master. His fellows hunch back. There is one inevitable act for John. He has been forgiven. He should touch his cap and pass. He holds his ground.

"Hope yo'-all 'll be feelin' better, too, Mr. Hade," he says. His hands are cold: his throat is dry and throbbing: his eyes catch the spike-like anger and amaze of these men who are like mists—their flesh—about the jet of their anger.

"Cloud, *move along.*"

Hade masters himself, and turns. He fears this ugliness, too. Does not he want to be the kindly and loving master? John moves. In the silent gap between the passing black man and the whites, lives a red sore that thought and time must swell.

John walked . . long rhythmic stride of the tall man walking. His moving traced the sore: it was the muttering men, it was the red road lengthening between them, it was he. Town, road, men, he, were the hot sore John carried . . growing . . as he walked to work.

Virginia Hade crossed toward him. She walking also to work.

Nazareth is dim in the blood-glint of John's eyes: blood of the hurt of his spirit prodded and branded and spiked by the world, by the sun. Women and men move angular, women and men stand in doors he may not enter as a man among them. They are all lost in a hush of red . . in his hurt.

But she, coming athwart the sorrow of his eyes, stands in his vision differently. Subtly, he is aware that she is different.

She is tall. Her gold hair lies in coils on her smooth brow. Her arms, sleeveless, swing gently as she walks toward him, the white dress lying in sweet intimacy upon the swell of her hips, upon the break of her breast.

His eyes, sharpened with hurt of other things, see Virginia Hade.

She smiles as she nods Good Morning. Her smile is an opening upon her face. The shutters of her eyes, of her mouth, turn in; she is all open, and John's look advances. Knowing it goes forward, John's look withdraws. But there, within the quiet of her face, it lives and it works.

He slackens his pace to avoid their being

even for a moment side by side on the hostile street. She hastens hers. He sees the crinkle of the skin at her elbow, at the nape of her neck: how fine her hair! He moves in a strange dissonance upon her path, upon the healing of her kindliness, while the hot red sore of the muttering men behind longs with him. . .

Mary Cartier! He sees her: she bakes bread in her crude oven. The cabin stands like a low sister of the trees. Her elbows are blue-black, the gums of her mouth are stained: she is a fleck of night, fair yet misplaced upon this rioting funnel of bright day in which John, walking, falls. Mary is the night. Singing. Miss Hade, outdistancing him, has disappeared in the office door. The road is gravel. Turmoil and Mary within him.

John is stopped. Eyes of a man, fixed near him, hoist his own sidewise. Judge Hade is at his shoulder: the lean and wooden elegance of Judge Hade like a sign at his shoulder.

"Good mo'nin', Judge."

"Good mo'nin', Lank. I have been walkin' by yo' side all of this street. An' yo' didn't see me."

He gives these words with a prophetic dryness. John feels the ominous threat of the knowing beneath them.

"I've watched you, nigger," they say, *"I've watched you lookin' at my daughter. How dare you look at my daughter? Nigger, that look in yo' eyes means murder in our land. How dare you, nigger, look so hard at my daughter that you forget to salute the white man at yo' side?"*

"Beg pa'don, sah." John answers the words and their meaning. . . Cold, smooth like ice, the world shuts down upon John's eyes as his mouth smiles and his head bows. No red: this world is ice: it is a world in which no living thing can grow; it is a world that shrivels and that stiffens; it is a world where life like fire breaks out, passionate, isolate, burning hungry holes in the dark sheet of death.

John goes to work.

THE office of Judge Hade and of his daughter is a high frame room with doors upon the garden. Its lacquered pine smells sweet.

Virginia sits at her desk and lays her hands upon a pile of letters. Her head is high, her throat throbs visibly: her eyes gaze through the doors to the low aisles of trees and bring to her white throat the impact of their sight: negresses picking fruit are darkling lights, shifted and sprayed by some fantastic screen. Through the green aisles, under the blue of the sky, within the rigid pine frame of the door, dark women flow and undulate. Virginia's hands lie stiff upon the pile of letters.

In the threshold at her side stands her father and looks at her gaze that has no room to know him.

He enters at last: shuts the door. He crosses and shuts the door through which her eyes have brought their burden back. Eyes of man, eyes of girl, meet compressed in the warm room, strike at each other. (Doors shut are periods . . putting a stop . . demanding that there be a stop. . .)

"Why shut the doors, when it is Indian summer?"

"You were dreaming. You'd better work."

"Have you any complaint about my work here, sir?"

"No, daughter. Why, of course not!"

"Then don't bother about doors."

She is up. She opens the door that faces her: it rasps against the room's compression.

Judge Hade sinks in the armchair and lights a long cheroot.

"What's the matter, this mo'nin'?" He levels his eyes along the black cigar: his eyes are there, hard beyond the glow, like little beasts.

"Matter with whom?"

"With everything! I tell you, the town's astir. Can't be Reverend Dill's preachin'. He couldn't rouse a nigger. An' the niggers . . what's the matter with them? Mutterin' . . stirrin'. . . An' the whites? What's come?"

She shrugged her shoulders: her hands still rigid upon the pile of letters.

Judge Hade puffs.

"Can't be just 'cause a nigger fell in the bay, last night. Can't be religion. Can't be the weather. Can't be hard times, fo' the crops are good. Peanuts might 'a' been better. But cotton, oranges, 'taters, nuts. . . What is it?"

"What about *you?*"

He drilled his little eyes again down the vision of his cheroot.

"Do you find anything wrong with yo' father?" he asked rhetorically.

She smiled: her hands, released, mechanically sliced with a long blade the envelopes before her.

"No, dear. . . But since it's *you* who feel it . . ."

"What do you dream so for? What were your eyes awandering out yonder for, when I came in? . . Do you know, you didn't see me standing there in the door for the longest time?"

She worked, now, swiftly.

"That long smart black . . Lank Cloud . . he was behind you comin' in to work."

Her hands, smoothing out orders, give a jerk.

"And he was looking at you, Virginia . . like you was lookin' out at those orange trees."

"How do you know it was like?" Her

lips were red and full, but a faint twist sharpened them, so they seemed gaunt.

"He walked the whole street alongside of me . . from Miller's to the door. He was so busy lookin' at you, he didn't see me, neither."

"Neither?"

"Like you didn't . . lookin' at those girls."

"O——"

For a moment she worked mechanically. The burden of her father's words gradually bore in on her and stopped her. She looked up.

"Father," she said, "you're the one that's sick . . you and Bob and the whole lot of you men. Why can't John Cloud look at what's before his eyes, if that 'what' happens to be me? Why can't I gaze out of my door just because there are dark girls in bandannas with low-cut open waists, singing and picking fruit? What are you men afraid of?"

"Daughter, you're smart. Smart enough to run this business by yourself. That I allow. But you-all ain't smart enough to run the South."

She repressed her answer with a smile.

"There's a whole lot of things you don't know about niggers. And God forbid you should! There's a whole lot of things you don't know about white girls . . about yourself, Virginia. And God forbid you should! That's what we men are here for."

"O it's maddening. And it's tiresome, too." She dropped her paper knife and beat her fists on the desk. "I'm no child. I'm twenty-four. I've got as much education as you have, Father—and of a far better crop. I know a whole lot more than Bob or James or any of your cronies. What's the matter? What are you afraid of, I repeat? Yes—*you* afraid of? The darkies know their place. Do you know *yours?* The darkies love their place. They're a lot happier and better off, I sometimes think, in their place than we in ours. But so it is, at any rate. We're here: they're there. It's you, with your fanatical obsessions——"

Judge Hade rose and tossed his cigar into the cuspidor.

"Go on thinkin' so, daughter. Go on thinkin'. May nothin' never come to change your mind, about the folly of us menfolk's care. That's what we're caring for. . ."

He spoke solemnly, quiet. He impressed her, speaking. He stood above her, silent, and his hand, upon her nervous shoulder, quickened them to one. The world came in through the open windows, through the open doors, through the senses open of this man and this girl: one within Nazareth.

World . . of Nazareth: worlds of Nazareth speaking:

—I cannot forget you, Niggertown. Night and day you glower. Night and day you shout and laugh, you sing and sway and groan. Always there beside me, Niggertown. Beside my birthright, within my mind like a shadow alive.

—Whah is yo' sister, blossomin' Dixie lan'?
Whah is de sister ob yo' sun and rain?
Yo' sun am smilin' an' yo' rain weeps warm.

—I walk on soil, and I need soil to live. But earth stays in its place. I plow earth, I scatter seed, I harvest. Upon the willing earth I place my house. Through the willing earth I run my roads and my rails. You stand up. You shout! You lift your arms, and the gleam of your eyes breaks in my twilight rest. You are earth too: and like the earth I need you. Within you I must sow my food and upon you make my ways. Yet you stand up! You shout . . .

—*When de sun goes down on Dixie lan'*
Mah dusky love shines in de welcomin' night.
Her voice am cool as de melon
An' her han's am sweet as de grape.
Upon her breast I lays an' dreams
Like in de sweetest balsam bed o' de Spring.

—How can I rest in you when you stand and shout? I am weary with whiteness. To rule, to be civilized and chaste; you do not know what weariness it is. My woman yearns toward me in hunger, I am spent. All the world waves in darkling circles about my white uprightness, I am spent. I must lean down on you, earth, lie in you. O you are warmth and power,

I am spent. Your pools draw my blood: your red soils blanch me dry. I must lie in you! But you who are my earth stand up and shout! How can I rest in you? how can I shut my eyes?

—*Leave me alone . .*
Don' you see we is lovin'?
Leave me alone . .
Don' tell me nothin'.
How kin I listen to you
When mah love's lips
When mah love's arms
When de soft breast ob mah love
Closes roun' me like de earth
. . all laughin' flowers
Comes roun' me like de air
. . all smilin' breeze.

—All the world's color: and I must hold my pride against the world. Pride is white. History is white. The Christ is white. Honor is white, and birthright. All else . . color. The sky and the sun and the stars, the trees and the thirsty soil: the eyes of my beloved and her lips . . color, color, foe to my high whiteness. And you fight me, and you suck me dry. Even my heart is color. In my mother's womb, I lay in blood: I was born, I was conceived in dark hot hours. I must be white . . and Christ is very dim.

—You-all don' count. Whah do you come in?
Ah kin raise co'n 'n' taters
Ah kin hitch mah mule
Ah kin still co'n likker
Ah kin love mah girl.
You-all don' count. . . Whah do you-all come in?

—Shouting, standing, rolling your hot eyes. Leave me be! Be earth! Don't break into my slumber and my dreams!

—You won' leave me be?
You won' leave me make mah cotton an' mah co'n?
You won' leave me love mah gal?
You low white trash!
You's a ghost, a hantin', a hantin' . . .
You won' leave me be?
What does a hant do but scah?
What does a hant do but spoil?
What does a hant do but make you look 'n' look?
Come, blossomin' lan', come, lan' of love and dream
Le's look away fum de white stalkin' ghost.

—I see you everywhere. Like blood. Like earth. You fed and cradled me, now you rise up, the angry flanks of a field, menacing, engulfing . . folding above my house! Like a mother you nursed me. You, my true mother. Now in the blue eyes of my love I see you darkly sing. I'll drive you out! Lie like a field! Get out of the eyes of my love!

—You won't leave me be?
What kin Ah do fo' yo'-all?
Tell me . . tell me;
Den perhaps yo'll leave me, leave me be.

—My love hungers, I am spent. What's that to you? Get out! The earth is a maze of fertile flowing flame. I am the Lord here, and I am white like Christ. Stay down!

—Whar are you? Why should I stay down?
O our village is singin' strong,

An' de crops is in,
An' de cotton's made,
An' de watermelon's ripe.
We goes rollin' into one
Down de red street to de moon
. . She stands dere like a melon in de sky . .
We goes rollin', we goes strong,
We is a great big thunderin' song!
Whar are you?
Whar a r e yo'-all?
White town? Da's funny. I's heard tell o' dat.
Dim, dim, dim, white town.
Why, sho! I's done heard tell o' dat.

—I'll crush you! If you're color and love, watch my white hate. I'll hold you! If you are seed and fruit, watch my white drouth exalt the dry well and the blind eyes of my women!

. . . worlds of Nazareth spoke.

Virginia Hade placed her hand upon her father's hand that rested at her shoulder. She looked up to him. Her black eyes, heavy-full, rose to the sharp gaze of the man, followed his eyes into the orchard: . . dark woman shapes dappling the rows of trees.

Daughter and father looked and heard together.

Part Three

NOON

NOON. The sun halts vibrant. Rays pour through the tremor of equilibrant heat. Animals, leaves, caked clay stand in the same suspension with the sun. Under the sun reaches the western sky that sun must fall through, die through into dusk. Now momently sun stands . . and the world stands with it.

A great Tent is beside the road: it is blue blaze in the sun: a sort of blazing ice: and its shadowed mouth breathes coolness. White Nazareth . . the stiff dark forms of the men, the pale rigidities of women walking, clasping code and prayerbook . . moves up the ruddy road, away from the bay that gleams like shattered steel, moves to the Tent, moves into its dark mouth. Nazareth fills the Tent and the Tent's cool shadows are bubbled out into the heat of the day. Filling with Nazareth, the Tent fills with heat. Shadows, crowded out, have no place to live: they die.

The Tent fills with the shadows of men and women: heat runs within their clothes: these shadows are hot. Mouths give forth frictioned song and word . . black heat: the eyes are dark, holding within an inward clarity that presses, presses, and the eyes that must hold back are hot.

The mouth of the chief hymn-singer shuts pursed. His eyes study the crowd with a prose canniness. He has arranged a quiet with his voice. The preacher steps forward, happy and at home in this manufactured quiet. His yellow hands . . "Let us pray." . . signal, spread out, and his eyes turn up, turn inward, and his mouth, grinding words, makes a sort of circular tension that conjoins the yellow bookrest before him, the yellow platform beneath him, the supine crowd that the Tent's blaze yellows: he and the wooden world he steps upon are one. . . White Nazareth in heat under the blazing ice of the Tent is happy in its wooden unison.

The Tent of Revival is a furnace. The fire in the sky has begun to slide, slide down: but the smolder of Nazareth at meeting rises. The Tent of Nazareth is a furnace with piddling outlets. *Thou Shalt Not Steal, Thou Shalt Not Lust, Thou Shalt Not Play or Dance* . . what outlets these for the thick smoke of Nazareth?

The wooden preacher and his Christ kindle the mass of the crowd. Passion snakes under laps, swirls up: passion murmurs within narrow brows: there is a larval silence that is flame . . stifling, curling, spreading within the ice-hot shadows of the Tent, and no way outward save these little holes, stopped long since by the vague smut of usage.

Thou shalt not. . . Thou shalt not. . .

O—O—O

LET ME FLAME UP

LET ME FLAME OUT

LET THE WORLD BURN FOR ME!

. . . The wooden preacher and his yellowed Christ are a tongue of flame that kindles.

VIRGINIA HADE has worked hard. She has walked home to luncheon. She has walked back to work. She has shut the doors of her office, shutting out the heat and the stir; and the ruminant questions shut in.

Knock.

"Come."

Cap in hand, John Cloud.

"Yes, John?"

"Pa'don me, Miss Virginia. It's pow'ful hot!"

"Hotter than all summer."

"You-all fo'get, perhaps, Miss Virginia. Often we has our hottest days in de Fall."

"That is so, John. One forgets."

"I suggests, Miss Virginia: we-all'd better let the pickers knock off."

He says no more. He is keyed to her own intelligent perceptions. They understand their workers. They two conduct this business of picking and preserving fruit. Isolate, uncommunicant, they two . . white girl, black man: boss girl and servant man . . move jointly like two parts, dumb to each other, indispensable, of a machine.

She nods.

"Let's all quit, John. What with the heat, and the Revival. . . You got Revival too?"

"Next week, Miss Virginia."

"Good! Let's all quit. Let's call it a Holiday. . . And John, could we . . just so's they pay for this . . could we have 'em an hour earlier, Monday, in the cool?"

"Sho'ly, Miss Virginia. Ah'll tend to dat. Good afternoon, Miss Virginia."

He turns and the door is shut: it does not shut her ears from the pace of his moving down the gravel walk.

The fire in the sky slides down
Nazareth fire mounts

Virginia resolves a motion from her moods. Between two windows . . long *espagnoles* draped in chintz . . there is a mirror. Her' face stares at her eyes. —What is the matter? Heavy eyes, dark and deep beneath the froward gleam of her light hair. She touches her brow: wan, feelingly it holds like a shell the clamor of some sea. Her lips move faintly, she draws them in and feels upon them myriad starting pains. Blood would jet out from this fullness held by her lips. Her eyes . . she stares within her eyes. There is a question in her eyes: what is it? There should be an answer too. Her eyes pulsate and burn as her eyes' gaze strikes in question at her eyes.

She shuts them. She stands in swaying blindness at the window. The women with open waists are gone: the orange trees are alone. The sky is far above. A cat skulking along the corridor of trees sets low the somnolent earth. Trees breathe in a stiff peace. The sky that nourishes with flayings of white heat cuts under the smart of her shut eyes in tiny crystals.

She opens her eyes. She puts on a bonnet: spreads a parasol: goes out. She walks up the baking street. The clay in striant measure responds to the heat rays, casts a lyric tension back into the air where the flexed waves are swirling between the vertices of sun and earth. Few persons pass Virginia. It is the last great day of the Revival. What moves on the street, moves as she, up toward the Tent.

She stands before the Tent. Her face is shaded by the parasol that casts a silken sheen against her eyes. Through the waved air, the Tent is pulsant. Its bulging flanks dip and yearn up: the earth line wavers underneath: pegs holding it with ropes are taut and angular like tugging heads, stubborning away, swelling the Tent against the dominant earth that runs and twists and quavers up and down.

Holding the parasol, Virginia steadies her wrist. Voices within clumsily grope for unison, rise hoarsely one. A gaseous heat seems to hold up the Tent. The posts tug taut with fragile rope against the swell of voices, against the waves of the earth. . .

Flame of the sky falls down
Flame of Nazareth mounts

Virginia turns away.

Judge Hade and his son bear down upon her turning. Leisurely sure, they walk toward the Tent. They are part of it already. They are part of that which brought it there, which swells it to life. Smiling sure particles they are of its heat and its longing, moving to join their flesh to its smug will.

"Well, daughter. Glad you left work early. Come."

They are held up by her vertical will.

"I am not going in."

"Not going in?"

Her brother studies her with a sharpness that cuts her spirit. Sweet pain comes of her brother.—His love is strong.

"Where are you going, sister?"

"For a walk . . now that you ask about it."

"Not comin' to Meetin'?" Judge Hade is perplexed. How can one choose to walk on a hot afternoon? There is no room in his mind for this event of being perplexed by his daughter. A flood of conventional reasons . . all passing, all proper . . come to his rescue. He is ruseful, knowing. He assumes a jest.

Virginia goes on: "I was there last night—up to the church. I don't like the Reverend Dill, any more than the Reverend

Spruce. He's half dead, seems to me. His voice sounds like a rotten canvas ripping."

Judge Hade laughs. "Come along, dear."

"No. I said I was going for a walk."

"Alright, then. Go." Bob has no ruse. His harshness beats against her heart. —I hate you! But his harshness is love, and she is glad for this. —Sweeter than the courtly way of father.

"Watch out where you wander."

She is tall, she looks level at her brother's eyes. Beside them both, she feels her father: his haughty shoulders droop, his slender frame is dry. But Bob is not drooping, and she is not dry. Her father's eyes peer out like strangers on this clash, from the cold cave of his thoughts.

"Bob, why do you insist on talking to me so? I'm not only older than you, and a whole lot wiser: I'm old. I'm getting old."

—Deny it! deny it! ". . Old enough. . ." He merely shrugs away.

"Old enough," Judge Hade breaks in, "to know that it is nonsense to take a walk on an afternoon like this. Madness——"

"O let her have her whim." Bob's tolerance like a treacherous spark makes a flare of her spirit. *—I'll have it! I'll have it. Any whim I want. . . God, if you knew, you with your nigger whores, what whims I want!*

"Madness it is!" The elder man fumes and is at last at ease with this chance of a gesture. There is a heat in his words, as if unconscious he was taking part in the silent dialogue before him. "Madness, in such heat! And the niggers off from work, roamin', roamin'."

"Well, I'm off from work, too. Can't I roam also? Can only niggers roam? Can only niggers sing?"

Judge Hade points eloquently to the Tent.

"You can sing there."

Virginia turns, takes once more the plethoric white blotch within her gaze. Nausea in her throat. With a releasing shake of her head, she turns again away: the nausea dims. She sees these brittle strangely static men within a mellow world. One, all brittle. One, already brittle beneath the flow of his youth. The Tent is loathsome white: a mucilaginous sack holding a spider's eggs . . myriad black live spots that will crawl, that will spread: *—Let me out!* She sees these men, and they and the thick sack of the spider and its eggs stick in her flesh.

—My flesh. Their hard thrusts pry at her flesh. *—My flesh!* Stir her, hurt her. Not thrusts, caresses she needs! *—My men folk.* They love me, and they know . . never for-

get . . the sweet love flesh I carry (vainly, vainly) through this passionate world.

She smiles. —Stiff fools that thrust, that pry, that don't know how to caress. She takes their hands, one in each one of hers.

"Dears," she croons at them;—big clumsy boys, "now run along to meeting. And forget me. I'm going where it's *cool.*"

JOHN CLOUD seeks the cool. His thoughts grind in deadlock, he seeks the cool from his thoughts.

The road meets the air. The waving heat, the undulous land break cool upon his brow. His eyes drink like a cool draught in this world wanton with autumn.

Simple world. The simple's the cool. Complexity is hot. Color and shade and light lie peaceful in this world, sharing it fairly, making it the world.

Like a great jugular the road bleeds spanning up the hill. John climbs. On the high level it forks. A stone wall in the juncture, tufted with wild grape, clamps a cotton field.

John leaps the wall and stands within the field. The stalks, black, thrust from the red earth. The cotton squares gleam bronze beneath the fluffing white of the flowers. John takes a boll that is desiccate and nude. He picks from it the devastating bug . . color of mold, angular, with vast proboscis: a miniature chimæra . . the boll weevil.

It stands greenish upon the loam-hue of his palm. He holds it carefully. Its ugly nose stings at his skin. He walks with it to the stone wall and sits down.

Land falls away. The sun bounds swiftly: the sky bounds with it. The rolling earth, fume of field and cypress grove and roof, runs pacingly along to the high marge where the land dips pine-clad into sea. All moves alike with the sun. A stillness swathes the world: a singing resolute measure that falls down, leaps up . . marked by the sun and the swaying trees. . .

John cannot hold himself. He falls along. Gentle and simple falling: falling of all color into the womb of white. He falls along, save his eyes only that hold a pause against their vision and make his mind the space that is the dissonance of thought.

The weevil pricks at his palm. He looks at it. His eyes are focused to the sun. This dirty living spot within his palm and thumb stands against the sweep of the whole world. Its tiny hardness, its dissonant prick in his flesh are like his thought that bites upon his view. John's head wavers in the alien sense of a weevil pricking his skin, and a thought his sight.

His thumb presses, presses. From the bug's frail carapace oozes its jet of life. And a smear, colorless, of death lies on the lovely humming afternoon. The sun tips the sky as it falls: the houses spew discord: the spanning roads bind pain upon the wistful land. And the land sinks slowly to the bay like a darkening failure.

John stands up on the stone wall, his feet in the ripe grapes. His hands are high above his head. In his eyes, Mary Cartier bakes her endless bread that is the color of earth, that flame has blacked unto the color of earth. A white hand, a white arm, slender and shrill, pushes Mary away into her oven. At the white arm's pit, a fringe of hair is golden: John smells it, it smells sweet like honey and manure. But delicate. Virginia Hade's black eyes flash with the arm that pushes Mary into her oven of clay.

John's hands brush his eyes. He walks. He knows where he is walking. . .

. . . . . .

Aunt Martha's cabin is almost lost in the corn, the cotton, the fig trees and the cane that crowd disheveled all about its bareness. A cabin over-ripe like a blue fig: its thatch roof falls, its slender porch-posts split, the windows squint awry upon the forward patch of yellow ochra blossoms.

Aunt Martha sits in a broken rocking chair upon the porch, and smokes a black clay pipe.

"Howdy, son; howdy, son," she calls in a voice timbred like a bell.

"How yo' feelin', Aunt Martha?" John lounges up and sits on the steps at her feet.

"O, fine. Fine, son." The clear bell voice . . "Ah cyan't complain. When yo'-all thinks," the phrases come forth swift and saccadely, ". . when yo'-all thinks o' de worl' 'n' how come us niggers ain't no better now, nor when we was slaves . . whah Ah cyan't complain. How *you?* Ah gets mah 'baccy an' mah co'n. De weevil, he ain't hurted none too much. An' de roof's patched. How *you?* Ah ain't complainin'."

He looks up, smiles at her. She smiles at him, holding her hot pipe in her hard black hand. Her face is round. No flesh lies between the blue-bronze skin and the bone. The broad mouth is black, the teeth grinning at John are white as the white of her eyes in which the darkling pupils gaze and peer.

—I wanted to see her. Why? I wanted to look an' see ol' Aunty Martha!

She watches his disquiet, quietly. The hair on her head is a cap of dusted wool. And beneath it the drawn high cheekbones, the arched nose, the firm stressed jaw stand bell-like as her voice.

"Well, son: three times Ah'm tellin' you: How yo'-all?"

"Well, Auntie: ef you ain't complainin', ken I?"

"Sho, son, sho!" Her bell laugh: "Complain ef yo'-all feels dat-away. Complain. Et'll do yo' good. Complain to yo' ol' Aunt Martha."

John Cloud smiles and stirs and is a little ashamed.

"When Ah sees yo' laughin', de complain' in me—why, it jus' lights out like a grasshopper."

She leans and shakes her hand, clasping the pipe, at him.

"Son: da's a look in yo' eyes Ah hates to see."

" 'Tain't so easy fo' to chase away a look."

"No, son. Da's so."

"Easier fo' to kill a weevil."

She rises from her chair.

"Fo' dat . . fo' de look in yo' eye . . yo' got to pray!"

"What's yo' see, fo' sho, Aunt Martha, in mah eye?"

"Ah sees de white look in yo' nigger eyes!"

She stands above him. Her hand is so close, his eyes feel the harsh glow of the pipe it clasps. Her fingers, blue-streaked, take its heat like stones.

"Son," she says, "it's de Lo'd brung you heah. Ah ain't a livin' a hun'erd yeahs o' weepin' in dis valley ob Death fo' nothin'. It's de Lo'd what keeps me heah . . an' keeps mah co'n patch an' mah cane patch sweet: 'n' makes mah cotton fo' me: 'n' sends you heah."

"Ah believes that, Aunt."

"Yo' better! Son," she brings her sizzling pipe almost against his eyes, "son, de Lo'd, he's *black!* Don' you nebber min' dem skulkin' nigger preachers. Wha' do dey know? Ah says . . an' Ah says it alone . . Ah says it spittin' in de face ob all de preachers in de Zion Church: de Lo'd, he's *black!* De Lo'd, he's de color of earth, he's de color o' de skies when de sun ain't paintin' 'em wid his white-man colors. De Lo'd, he's *black!* An' son, what he hates in a nigger, what he won't nebber fo'give, am de white look in yo' eyes."

"Who put it dere? Ah didn't."

"Dis hyah night, son," her hand goes up and down, the dim smoke of her pipe swings like a censer's, "dis hyah night, Lank John Clou', yo' tak' yo' Mary! She'll wash de white fum yo' eyes." Her rising voice turned subtly into song. "Tak' her, chil', hol' her close: paint her lovin' flesh all over yo' pale heart. Do lak' Ah say. She'll wash de white fum yo' eyes." A bony palm went out, and John pressed a dime in it.

The old woman nods. There is no sense of thanks within her eyes. She clasps the coin, as she breathes the air of the Lord. And her deep eyes roll solemn, her voice speaks clear behind the censer-smoke of her black pipe.

"T'night, son . . dis hyah night. Tak' yo' savin' Mary. Do lak' Ah say."

. . . . . .

John strode square into Niggertown. Trees laid their screen of green between the blaze of afternoon and him. He thought of the old women whom he knew. —Why do I want to see them? Why don't I want to see my mother?

—Ol' women wise: ol' women ready to go
back in de earth.
Yo' words are earth, yo' wisdom is de
earth.
*What do you know, ol' women, of de
sun?*
Ol' women wise, ol' women ready to go
back in de earth.
Mother-women, woman who is mah
mother. . .
I don' carry yo' wisdom along, when I
dream:
Fo' it is heavy, ol' women, it is dark, ol'
women . .
Heavy 'n' dark like de earth!
*What does it know, ol' women, of de
sun?*

He wants to see his mother. Very strong, a weariness presses on his brow and his neck, and his throat. His body is released, his head is bound. He fights . . walking straight toward her . . to be free of the want of his mother.

—I'm a fine lad, spendin' my afternoon
Dreamin', an' visitin' ol' women!

Mary Cartier?

—This is the way that leads to meetin' her. What if I did?

—I'll look at you, Honey. I'll hold you quiet in mah eyes, till I ken look at you.

Her home lies near his trail. He stands at the hedge of holly by her house. The ground is smooth with spray of cedar and cypress. John stands, and there must come a call from his thoughts: Mary comes out to him: her bare feet singing on the needle-floor, and her face vibrant in the leaf-screened sun.

The placing of her hands out toward him is an echo (softer, no less clear) of the bell voice of Aunt Martha. She was metal, naked clanging glint of bronze. Mary is firm like a bud, like half green wood with sap running up. She stands there, hands held forth. As he comes near, she is to him a glade in the woods in which the sun shoots clear to its deep of bright flowers.

They clasp hands.

"Ken you come in, John?"

"No, Mary: I'm walkin'."

Her hands fall and her face. Her eyes look up.

"Ken you come back fo' supper?"

"Sho, Mary. Thanks. I'll come back."

She laughs:

"Then, don' go too far, John. Yo' might fo'get to come back."

"I won't fo'get to come back."

"Then don' go too far."

She watches him go. Her eyes fill with a wistful knowing: but her mouth is young and it smiles, her head tosses challenge to her eyes with their dark knowing. Only her hands faint, as she cups them hard on her breasts:

"Then . . don' go too far!"

Flame of the sky falls down
Nazareth fire mounts

DOWN. . .

Live oak, mildewed, lean upon each other. Moss reaches gray gaunt fingers down to his way. Wood seeps with phosphorescence. Tree frogs and fungus and a startling orchid thicken forbiddance. In the black maze of branches, mistletoe gleams a ghost. The trail ruts along a stream, sharp bamboo bars it. Everywhere sunlight sicklies in the pale moss streamers, hardening, drying to dark.

John's mind is blank. He sees the thickish congeries of wood moss flower, feels shifting the isolate soil and the dim light sky where a sun falls, falls . . but life within him has annulled itself. He is a lock of conflict: he is naught.

Up . . .

The wood is lighter. Oak streams its moss now almost gayly: moss is a wistful song of the gnarled trees between earth and sky, reaching for both. The sky is nearer, the earth is nearer sky. And sky wings through the resilient dense of green, carrying crystal pelts of bay-salt mixed with sun.

Up . . .

Bamboo, oleander, camphor, all the lesser life fall back from the approach to the bay and its winds. Cypress, dwarfed, knotted, here . . and thicker pines. The brackish boil of mud and clay is gone. Here is a floor serene . . strewn needles . . for John walking light. He knows what he will do. His body thirsts, he is parched with the hot feet running myriadly upon it of his struggles, of his loves and hurts. His body thirsts: let it drink!

He stands on the land's high edge. Precipitous the soil tooths down to a gray sub-ledge that slides out like a tongue in the bay. The water sleeps. Blue-purled it murmurs out beyond land's shade: sun strikes it golden. The water deepens. It is a sheen, ruddy and rose and red, spreading to mist before it ends in the horizon. No boat flecks its somnolence. At John's shoulders, stand the woods, rising in spaced strength. No hand is here. No white palm has scooped this fairness into possessive drouth. All is wide, all is free. The sun is a free dance in the heaven: earth and water rest sweetly in John's mind, his own . . their lovely breadth . . balming the sores of his soul.

John looks down. —*Danger.* He laughs. If he leaps far out, he'll miss the scoop of the ledge. Water's deep beyond. . . An ecstasy is air, kissing his arms, his shoulders, lipping his chest as he flings off his shirt. An ecstasy is air, clasping his thighs, his stomach, his legs. John stands naked in the clasping air, between earth and water . . drinking the air he needs. His body is bronze, firm-surfaced over its muscles. Hairless, it gleams like a molding of the sun. His head is small. Broad shoulders, faintly rounded in a ridge of strength, taper down swiftly to the slender waist. Here, the dark flesh is tender. The arms are a living metal. The ankles are lean. He stands in the cool ecstasy of his release from clothes . . from men. A tremor, like a warm dew, rises in his body. His hands go high. The legs flex sudden in a rhythmic brace. He arches into the air. Slowly, his head curves forward . . down. A flaw of the tree screen lets in the sun: tongue of flame on his bronze back. He cuts the water fleckless and is lost beyond the purple ledge. . .

Through the parting of the tree screen, Virginia Hade steps forward. The smooth floor under the spanning trees is kind to her feet. She sits under a wide live oak, spreading her skirt. The bay is a golden shimmer through the trees. The floor is a fending brown that holds the bay far off.

SHE has walked, she has walked. In her head murmurs, sudden strokes like steel on hollow pipes. But a cushion of disregard bars the place that noises from the place that could hurt. Her feet alone in the hot press of the day have the balm of pain. The sub-soil of the earth, bare in the roads that cut beneath the loam, parches her feet and makes her walk the more. In Virginia's head murmur and metal strokes urge savagely toward the place where they could hurt:—I want to feel up there, I want to feel. What keeps me from feeling? So her feet press hard: they feel: through the red day she carries her white world with her.

A great jugular is this road, bleeding up the throat of the hill. She climbs. The earth is a spread fume of field and cypress and roof. It rolls away to the far pine marge, it dips swift to the sea. Its running freedom pours against her brow. She does not stop at the hill's level height. The road forks. No choice. She goes down with the road toward Niggertown.

—I feel sorry for myself. That is strange! . . With the ease of her feet, down, down, and the pouring of the land toward the bay, she has thoughts.

She knows how quiet-quick this pity for herself may turn to rage. Rage to what? Rage against something. The red road falls, and her white feet fall with the road, toward Niggertown. Pity moves with her down against the black. In her high head, pity: against those low heads, rage.

—Why do I fall toward you, this afternoon? Why does the road run easily toward you? And the white pride of her brow, why does it not protect her?

—Pity for me? Anger for them. She

walks with a pale glimmer in her mind like a door opening.

—O you have so much! *Low down. . .* You dumb and dull, we talk like you. And we sing your songs. And wherever we look, be it at Christ himself, your color's in our eye. *Low down. . .* In the quiet of our evenings at home, you are there. My feet wander in pain, toward you they wander. Pity for me. *Low down. . .* Pity for me! I'll not feel sorry for you blazing niggers. You grow out of the soil. Your flesh stays sweet in the dank flames of the South. We wage a pallid fight, an ugly——there you are, blazing in ease, in truth, against our lies. Pity for me!

—When you sing and play, you forget us.
Our play does not forget you.
When you plow and sow, you forget us.
Our hunger does not forget you.

When you reap and eat, you forget us.
  Our ease cannot forget you.
When you sleep, you forget us.
  Our sleep has dreams. . .
    There was a Mammy rockin'
    There was a brown breast warm
  Our sleep is dreams of you.

—Pity for me. God damn you, nigger world! We have the brittle man-made toys, O yes. Laws, clinking coin, hard deeds, O yes. Stone banks, stone churches . . resting all on soil, resting on you! Pity for me whose feet sink weary down a bloodred road loathsomely toward niggers.

A little cabin under the dense squares of two chinaberry trees held her. —It's lovely! The trees had a symmetry like painted toys. And the cabin's low blue grace beneath the opaque foliage gave to her eyes the sense of faëry. A voice called out. And a voice answered.

"Viola, whah's de chu'n?"

"Un'er de co'n crib, Ethel. I done hide it thah, fum dem nosey hogs."

"Un'er de co'n crib?"

"Yes, hon'. Un'er de co'n crib."

A song fringed their words. Now with the words done, song took them altogether. One woman scrubbing, one woman churning, sang within the glow of a dark cabin. Virginia went along. Women were seated in the shade of trees; women were nursing on rickety rocking chairs in the shade of propped thatch roofs. Women were mending. Children lay about . . black boys, with gleaming eyes skin teeth, played fondly close to half-nude girls whose bodies shone like ebony in rags. Wide mouths parted and voices came like subtle brass, polyphonous and welded in a simple rhythm that the trees stanchioned and the cabins based, and the roving hogs and goats grazingly measured. Young brass of youth, warm wood-notes of the women and the draw of resinous strings . . where a man joined in, who sat at ease with his woman . . merged upon Virginia's walking to a song as dense as the earth. Song and earth sustained her in a strange bitterness of recognition.

They saluted her. Men, tipped back in chairs, straightened and touched their caps. Women looked up from their ovens and their wash. Children stared out from a bright wonderment and in their gaze resentment was already old.

The nigger world is a warm full beating music: a music mellow: the nigger world is a music filling the world from the trees right down to the earth. She walks alone in it. Upon its edge, her walking and her voice of calm salute are a white silence. The nigger world encaverns her salute, engulfs her whiteness.

—***Dey let a nigger drown***
Dey looks an' he drowns an' dey smiles

. . A stone of Hate hardens within the music.

"Howdy, Miss Hade." . . "How you-all?" . . "How you feelin'?"

"Howdy?" She smiles.

Hate! Hate!

—Dey let a black boy drown.

. . She is white, fringing this pent music.

She is faint.

A cabin stands alone. At one side holly, bamboo, fig trees and the high grille of an orchard. Upon the other side, the impervious cypress roof and the sun beating on its copper-green. The cabin plot between lies in bare heat. It is jeweled there, vibrant, within its matrix. A dark girl stands unconscious in the sun. She is turned toward the wood. A rake in her crossed arms flexes her shoulder up toward the profiled chin. The heat is shrill. It gives to the cabin background a stony brilliance upon which she stands like a flat carving. The line from brow to nose is straight. The lips are full. The hair rounds her face like subtly carven wood. Narrow shoulders point before and behind and her hands are upturned, and laid upon her breasts.

She hears steps. Turning, she moves from the plasticity of dream into this turmoiled day. She sees Virginia.

"Won't you come in, Miss Virginia?"

Virginia, faint, veers through the wooden gate. Mary Cartier places a chair for her on the porch. Virginia sinks into it. There is another chair. But Mary stands.

"You don' look well, Miss Virginia."

"O—I'll be alright."

Virginia wants her to sit too. She does not know how to frame this strange desire. —Is it the heat makes me want her to sit too?

Mary has gone and returned. "Jus' a

swaller, Miss Virginia." The water is pungent cool as the soil is pungent hot. Virginia looks at it in a rebellious longing. In her eyes, the water turns to a slakish brown. Nausea creeps up. She sets the water of the nigger world aside and the hard black hand receives it, carries it away.

They are two girls: one stands in rhythmic ease, the other in the chair of her who stands, is suffering.

"Jus' been fo' a walk, Miss Virginia?"

Mary is sure she has come upon some errand. Strange errand it must be. But a strange day too. The world is restless. The summer is dying hard. The trees hold a secret. At ease, her flexed hips forward, she looks at the white Mistress, and she waits.

Mary wears a shirt of soft dun cambric. At the throat it is wide flared. In her leaning ease, the breasts, high and small, press up. Virginia sees their satin brown: sees the nipples red like coagulate blood upon the satin breasts.

—I am afraid of this girl!

She stretches out her hands.

"Mary," she says in a voice so strangely white it startles her. "I'm just out for a walk, dear. Really. And I'm tired. And you've given me a seat like a dear on your porch. Well—sit down, too. We'll chat a bit, till I leave."

Mary's swift smile is chased by her own hardened eyes. Her mouth shuts. Her hands flutter. "O no, Miss Virginia." She is suffering. "Ken I get you . . a glass o' milk? . . or some of our new plum wine? It's pow'ful good, Miss Virginia." Her smile wants to come back. But her eyes and mouth stay hard. —What delicate pain! Virginia feels before this exquisite anguish the need of her highest grace.

"Well," she stands, too. So she solves the problem.

She holds the girl's scared eyes. —I wanted you to sit down, Sister. Ain't you that? I thought of nothing else. What else is true? I am tired, and you helped me. Is it fair I can do naught for you?

Passionate and deliberate Virginia thought these words. And the scared eyes softened: a quavering smile like a blue flame warmed Mary's face. —She is suffering, now. But it is sweeter pain.

The two girls stand. Mary's body is bent a little backward. She has the message of Virginia's eyes. Upon her ancient life it steams and hisses like a fragile jet of water on a smoldering fire.

Sudden she comes forward. She flings her dark bare arms about Virginia's neck. The warm full lips press the pale ones. Then Mary steps back, freed.

They glow at each other. They could not sit together. But they could kiss! Virginia presses her an instant in her arms. She feels the breasts of Mary against her own, the lips of Mary on hers. She knows that she must leave at once. There must be no social strain to mar this perfect moment of communion. —Never before have I so needed all my strength, all my grace. Your power, girl, your grace . . call forth the height of mine!

"Good-by, dear." Even her hands do not go forward: even a handclasp would mar. "You've helped me," she says. "Thank you. I'm feeling well, now. Good-by." . .

Slowly, she turns through the wooden gate . . turns toward the cypress jungle: turns away from the kempt fruit-grove whence she could cut back so easily toward home. She walks fast . . she is gone.

Mary comes down once more from the porch:

Flame of the sky falls down
Flame of Nazareth mounts

and her mellow profile, her shoulders flatten against the naked heat . . peering away toward the sea, questioning. . .

—Why?
He went that way,
What moved him?
She went that way,
What moves her?
He and she
And I
An' the slidin' sun
An' Nazareth risin' risin'
Risin' flame? . . .

Her mind touches a truth far out from the frail grasp of her mind. Her mind is cool: cool sculptured grace she is against the jeweled afternoon. But her cool mind touches a truth.

She has crossed her palms flat upon her breast. And her head is turned: and the shoulders high cast up the delicate rondures of her neck, of her chin, the straightness of her brow cupped in the hair. So she stands, her cool mind touching a delirium of question: touching a world darkflamed where the man she loves and this woman who has kissed her disappear.

VIRGINIA has walked fast. Toward the bay where the airs come cool and free. Through the parting of the tree-screen, she steps out . . sweet running air! The floor is soft with needles goldensoft under the trees. Trees hold the sky up high, so the air can run. —How good it is here! She sits down under the wide live oak. She spreads her skirts, the cool air steals in. —If all of me could drink this running air! Impossible. She knows that she longs to cast off her clothes, to lie naked, to run naked in the world. Crisp needles will bite her, creep at her thighs. . . Never. Never. Why? She smiles. She seeks a solace she can have in the far strip of sea that hangs so cool out there between the day and the earth.

. . . . . .

John Cloud swims deep. His legs draw in, spread back: his arms . . drawn fingers tingling . . shoot ahead in the close world of water. Air is a sparking sheet above his brow. His eyes are open: water voluminous and convolved lies back from them. Beneath, the heavy ledge widens from purple into a dappled brown where the sun splotches fall.

He feels his body. The air in his lungs is like a white restraint holding him solid from this liquid world. The air is sweet in him and new: it will throb and murk and clot, then he must go up again to the dancing sunmotes lest the watery sheath clap in, break in upon his clean bronze body . Now, air is cool yet in him: he can swim still within the secret spread of sea life looming so inevitably vast beyond his eyes that life above, sparkle of sun, seems false. Foliage, magenta, chrysoprase, swirls in cornelian currents, stills in black depths. He can swim and know with his body gliding through the velvet dim the gladness of strength. The ledge lips in. The water darkens. A maw of black in which the sun is swallowed lies like a pressure underneath his breast. He plunges. The ledge incurves like the unfolding flesh of a woman loving. John's head floats wide-eyed in the lips of a cave that holds its blackness pure from sun-flushed water.

Wide-eyed: the water films his eyes and casts on them rolling up from the cave a spell. He is out of time, and he is out of space. The air in his lungs throbs, waiting. . . . . .

. . She is dancing. She is naked. She is black. No flesh between her gleaming skin and her bones. She is a spell of bones, rhythmed and swathed by the fire behind her. Fire stands in her eyes. Her eyes are holes: fire comes through. Fire cannot melt her bones. Fire enfolds them, fire lifts them into dance. She is dancing on John's brow. Feel her feet! She is dancing on John's chest. Her toes are scarlet! She is dancing on his groins. She is hurting. God! she hurts. . . *Come away!* . . . She is dancing on his groins. She is gone. But his flesh aches. Her feet have stamped and bitten him: have bound and wounded him. She is gone. But his flesh has caught her dance. In his belly, in his chest, on his brow, dances flesh that is he. Flesh of her who is fleshless and is gone. . . *Come away!*

The cave of unfolding lips opens, opens with the deep pressure of his stroke. There is a spread of field. . .

Cows stand lush. Sun casts a white flake of cloud on a grove of aspen. Aspen branches spray in bud. John lies on his back. His legs spread wide. And his mouth sucks the udder of a cow. It is soft and thick and haired upon his face. As he sucks, his great thirst grows. *Air! Air!* Sweet milk sprays down his throat, thickens and stifles in his throat. His breast is heavy with black clots of pain. Sweet udder presses his face: thickens and stifles. Udder and milk fold out, engulf his mouth and his eyes. The sun glints away, a flash of struck steel in the dark.

Like a speared fish, John turns belly up. Floats up, floats up. Myriad sunmotes, sparkling maddened stones spread a hard striking on his face. *Air!* He drinks it, floating. The gold stones melt, fuse . . into afternoon.

John swims slow strokes to the shore. He clambers free. The dimness pearls from his mind as the water from his flesh. He is free . . free of water, free like an insatiate dart through air. He is free resistlessly. But not afraid to be free. Too strangely full is the lunge of his clear self through air.

Self cannot hold self back so free and alone. He clambers up the ledge . . his clothes are up there, but he does not mount for his clothes. *High!* that is it. When he gets to the flat high pine-strewn floor, he will raise his arms, his arms will sing: *High!* He will take the highest tree on the cliff. And he will climb the tree. When he gets to the broad high branch he will raise his arms, his arms will sing: *High!* Up . . up. His body, clambering, is arched like a panther. Hands and feet master the stubborn way. His body, pearled with water, he keeps free of the soil.

At the edge, he rises . . slowly . . to his height: balancing, for his brow disturbs him with its thrusting freedom. The grove of trees and the smooth needled floor are awry to his gaze. They come to him refracted, as by water: a golden water that spilled jeweled motes upon the twisting trunks and the coiled earth. He is dazed. His nude skin at every pore drinks freedom, and his brow is quenchless drinking. Hereabout lies a strange pine bench, miracle and real, like the field in the cave and the wild lean woman who danced.

Trees . . common trees: but he notes that their roots have sense like clasping fingers, and their erectness is a subtle balanced thrust from their own muscled roots, like his erectness from his feet, from his thighs. The earth which the roots clasp, from which the trunks of trees stress gracefully is a treacherous flank: it veers, it shifts, it distends. Trees must balance wisely upon such a heaving floor. . . Under a tree sits . . skirts spread out . . a white girl. Her eyes like rods aglow thrust horizontal. She is not stranger than the cows and the dancer. He cannot see her quite so clear. In the shade. He comes forward to see her.

He stands very close above her sitting

with skirts outspread. He is naked bronze above her, within her eyes.

—Is she like the cave world?

He stands and watches her. She does not move. A heat comes from her. It makes his body cold. His hand touches his naked loin.

—*God! it is she God! I am naked before her!*

But he is free, and his self cannot fear his self, so free he is.

Her face also is pure of the shower of tormenting thought that breaks down dense from all about their world . . *the terror of this!* . . and cannot break within them.

He turns and walks away. The sense of the panic that should be his . . out there . . is a vague beating, an ineffectual rain upon the roof of his freedom. She is moveless. She is more moveless than the writhed trees that shade her. At the foremost pine, his clothes await him. He slips them on. His wrists are firm, his head is still. A blazing whiteness of reality floods all his body and his mind. He is quick and hard and sure in this writhed world. Each particle of self he touches, dressing . . his leg, his chest, his arm . . responds like a bell to the metal of his freedom.

He is real. He knows his body, dimensioned: its impeccable rightness. He knows it there, struck like a note on the bronzen bell of the world. He knows . . he is dressed:—*I am going to turn about.* I am going back to the white girl waiting for me.

—Distance to her my feet must pace is real. Real fades. I am there. She is you! At Virginia's side is a wide tree stump. John sits down.

—I have stood naked before her.

—He has stood naked before me.

. . . His body is a flame that has kindled them both, and is gone. They sit together.

She speaks: "You are happy. Your swim has made you happy."

She speaks again: "This has brought ease to me. Seeing you swim so free, seeing your fine body. . ."

She dwells half silent now upon her words: "I'd love to do that too. Run free. Ride free. Swim free. . . Be free, John, too." A whisper. Her eyes go with it warmly, meet his eyes. Fullness too hot constrains her. She is hard. "Why can't I too—— It's not fair, is it, John?"

The bond between them is warmer, is more drawing. Her voice scarce breaks the stillness of the day. Stilly the sun falls down the verdant roof: stilly the boughs stir, the earth sleeps.

"John."

He looks at her voice. But he is very hard, sitting beside her. Almost he is stern in this full knowing of the miracle of life: his self, his freedom, she. . .

"John, would you mind if I too ripped these things away and plunged in the water, and swam? . . Would you watch out for me, John? . . Would you keep off eyes——"

She smiles, and in her mouth is the mellowness of tears.

"I couldn't. I'd break my back. I'd break my heart too, John." Her eyes, black, leveled to his, dilate into a haze of gold. "You see, you're superior to me. You can do what I cannot."

In the quiet now, their hearts beat and they hear them.

He sees her throat, full in its tender shadows, throb with his heart.

"It's not a real talk, Lank John, if you won't say a word."

"There's a cave down thah . . an' a skinny witch that dances. The cows graze. . ."

"Down in the bay?"

"Un'er the water. I like to drowned,

dreamin', seein'. Did you see me go down?"

"No. I didn't really know you there . . but I did, I did . . not till I saw you come up gleaming. Then I knew I'd known. I saw a crouched dark thing. I wasn't frightened. It straightened up. It was you."

"Ah right near drowned. The witch woman, she danced on mah chest. An' a cow gave me suck. . ."

"I sat up here. . . That never happened to me."

"Other things happen to you . . that never happen to me."

She smiled. "Such wonderful things? I don't think so, John. I *know*. . ."

New calm between them. The warm bond throbbed less tense. It drew less taut. For they were closer, closer.

She laughed. Her laughter lay in him like a pied flowered Spring. He plunged his eyes and his mouth into her laughter.

"I *know*—I *know*. . . Because I'd give it *all:* all that I have, all that has happened to me: just to see that cave and those cows." She was wistful again. But her wistfulness lay confident: it rested in the man's eyes, in his hands. "Just to see that witch . . dance." She gazed hard at him, but she was close and her eyes did not hurt his own. *"I see her.* She's dancing now in your eyes!"

She looked away. She hid her face in her palms. Stillness.

"I ought to be afraid, I suppose, of that dancing witch."

"You needn't fear, Miss Virginia."

Her hands twitched, parted, with his words, as if the current holding them had ceased.

She looks up. Her eyes like strangers blink at the falling sun that stands within the eaves of the farthest pines. Chill comes to her eyes. And to him. They do not move. A hard dead planet looms: will it eclipse their day? John reaches to his pocket and brings out his knife. Her eyes, watching him, are warm again: gold-hazed. He takes a twig, he whittles, looking down.

She straightens her leg and lifts her skirt. John sees, not looking, her knee that is naked. The stocking is folded down and the white knee is dimpled. John's wrist veers as he whittles, keeps on whittling: he cuts his thumb. Virginia draws from the stocking a thin-blade knife. She smooths her skirt. John's blade is red with his blood.

She holds out her little knife.

"Let's exchange," she says.

Insanely, he examines the two weapons, gives to each the scrutiny that he would give in any bargain. His knife is large and clumsy. The handle is black wood. The single blade is thick and notched. He holds it, studying, in his hand with thumb and steel clotting red. Her white wrist rises before him. Within the tapered fingers a sheath of mother-of-pearl: white, blue-rhythmed like her hand, like her throat. And the useless delicate blade.

" 'Tain't a fair bargain," he judges slowly. "Not for you, and not for me, it ain't fair."

She places her hand still closer.

"Come! Exchange!"

His free hand moves and clasps her blade-clasped hand. As one, so joined, they rise up from the ground. They are close. Hand within hand, face to face, breath touching breath. Above their confronted eyes, their locked hands rise and the steel flowers up from their clasp.

His eyes fall from the knife. Her body is not tense like the steel: not hard. Within his hand, her hand is soft and warm. Within his eyes, her body is warm, breathing.

His hand, holding her hand with the steel blade up-pointed, loses the knowledge of her hand. Her hand is white, is flesh: her hand is woman. Her hand is leading down against the knife!

Her hand leads down to her. Her body, standing close beside his own, measures her ease against his stern restraint. Its glow draws him. Its molten pride is a call.

Clasping still her hand, his hand contracts. Hard. Harder. . . Her eyeballs harden and shrink . . are black harsh points. But still her body is beyond his clasp: he is possessed by it, he cannot grasp it. Within his eyes her body's moving forms invade him. He is transfixed, he is displaced and wracked and marvelously broken . . filled with this sweet unbearable trample of her flesh within his breast, within his heart and loins.

—*I am John Cloud. John Cloud!* His hand drops hers. Both of his hands fall limp.

"Will you exchange?" she whispers. In her voice, the voices of many wills collide to silence. For a moment she is his creature there: a sterile moment. For he obeys her: takes her knife, gives her his own crude blade. About the knives is darkness. He seeks to see her. *—I am John Cloud. Nigger.* He finds her face. Her features are drawn and hard as if his words for himself had struck her dead. . . Unreal face, all naked before his: it is like a forest in the high noon of summer stripped sudden of its leaves. . .

She sees him: unreal, too. In his eyes snow: his body is flame, but in his eyes snow. . .

John Cloud walks away.

Virginia Hade is alone. She looks: —With John's knife alone. The blade is stained. . . —With John's blood, alone. . .

Fire of the sky falls down
Flame of Nazareth mounts

The trees rise still: the earth floor is smooth. And the bayline, quickened by sun, is a quivering silver girdle at earth's loins.

Virginia sinks down and hides her face in her lap. She weeps. She stares up blinking at the bright strange day. Her cheek in her lap has pressed against the knife. It is soiled with blood. She feels the sticky smudge upon her cheek. She takes the knife and lays it on her brow. She presses hard, and her head sways:

—Pity! Pity me!

She drops the knife. —Am I loathsome? Is it loathsome to be me? She is calm. She looks at the wide tree stump where the black man was. She looks at his knife, at her side upon the ground. She takes the knife. Her two hands clasp it with impassioned vigor. She holds it tense and pointed to her breast. . .

—I am your world. You cannot break
from me.
Like a white frost I lie upon the earth
And the flowers are black.
I am proud. I am old.
Hollow brittle bones
Dare not dance.

—*I am myself.*
I am a vineyard heavy with grapes
Rotted.
I am a granary golden with grain
Rusted.
O splendor of my heart
Dry. . .
O vigor of my loins
Lone. . .

—I am your men.
In my brain a canker of remembrance
In my heart a waste of longing.

—*I am myself.*
Alone. . .

I am summer
I am sun,
Summer, seedless. . .
Sun, soil-less. . .

—I am your mate.
In my mind vacant straw.
In my house rotted wood.
Do not burn me! Do not burn!

—*I am myself*
Alone. . .
I am Spring
Alone. . .
I am love
Alone. . .

—I am your world. You cannot break from me.
I am your world. You cannot break from me.
Glory in me. Stanchion me! Defend me!

—*I am myself.*

—Fertility
Summer
Sun. . .
Madness of color dancing in my soil
Madness of Spring adance against my frost
Madness of love leaping against my law. . .
These are my Foe:
These are your Foe . .
NIGGER!
I am your world. You cannot break from me. . .

. . Virginia's arms are tense. "Can't I?" she mutters. "Can't I?" At her arms' length, the two hard fists clasp the inpointing knife. Her arms draw in. The knife cuts her waist: cuts her skin. The kiss of the steel is bright within her flesh. Her arms draw in. The blade lies like a tongue enfolded. Blood seeps out. The white waist has a heart of red upon it. Her arms are tense no more. Her head swims: white and adrift in a thickening dark she is: and is at peace. The knife falls to her lap.

—I am your world. You cannot break
from me.

Virginia rises slowly to her feet.

"I've cut myself," she says aloud. "What's that? One cuts oneself. . . The beach will take me home."

INTERLUDE

NORTHWARD the cliffs grow gentler and a beach, girdling land, swings smooth to Nazareth. In gullies that blind with their deep clay the sun like hot silk swaths, the streams of water yellow and trickle down. The beach narrows, widens: it is a mood of restraint, its variance the swaying of the struggle between the tumbling tumult of the land and the calm water. Here, Virginia walks.

—My walking home is my walking toward death. . . I know that. . . I walk fast.

—Virginia, Virginia, what horror is this in your will?

She knows herself with heavy steps walking clear beneath the cliffs: and the water deep in the afternoon lipping myriad ruddy lips and tongues up toward her.

—I am calm. Is it some greater frenzy?

The flesh wound of her breast sucks like a baby mouth. The air is cold at the smudge on her brow. —I am calm.

—Calmly I walk toward home.

—I am strong.

No doubt mars her.

With her wound, proudly she walks toward her wound's fulfillment.

The smooth beach has smoothed her.

The waters already freed from the low sun free her.

Sand is a harsh purity that grinds the mist from her eyes.

—I am up. I have been low and I am risen up. . . At last to your height, at last above you, Nigger. God, how have we suffered that they should be above us? Clean black you were. So you rose from the bay . . clean black flame: so you stood like a tree among the trees. *I murked you. I broke you up.* I'll save you yet, from the mud I made of you.

—Is this my walking home? John . . perhaps I'm walking home for you. You know what it means, my walking home? You know. The eyes of my menfolk upon me. You know. There'll be no mist in their way. They'll be a clear stroke too. That'll save you, John.

—We are the masters. And we mar our slaves. We muddy their well of strength. Save them, masters. There is a way to save them.

Virginia bears toward her drab white world, her thought is a streaming banner on the beach. Upon drab Nazareth she moves with her life: its splendor shall enflood the dirty town.

Her eyes are at ease: they are alone with their hard certainty. Cannot she spread the scarlet of her life like a sky on dim Nazareth?

The flesh wound at her breast hurts like an unfulfillment. She knows this hurt.

Her body, whole, often at night has hurt with this same suck of unfulfillment. The flesh wound at her breast is not new, it is ripe. It is the ripe red fruit of her old hurt.

—Can't I go back? Is there another way? But her feet do not slacken. She sees herself naked on the ground in his embrace. . . And then? That is a dimming too. A bastard way. It would go yellow like a bastard child through a dusk life. No way is clear, no way is clean save this she walks, bearing like flame on Nazareth.

—Can't I be sorry? Can't we be saved in pity?

"Pity me!" That was her cry, walking like twilight through the Nigger noon. Shame! She was twilight. —I am clean. I am all white at last. No pity for me. Pity for no one! Pity's a sun behind a murk of tears. In the unsullied noon of truth, no pity. Mud soothes. Mud soothes a sting. Pity is mud. . . She holds her hand to her breast. —Would I place mud there? . . walking toward Nazareth.

Sands widen. Low bay silent in the falling sun. Tangle of moss and rotted trees grays out at the drop of a gulch: and herself goldhaired with the scarlet mouth at her breast, her eyes like coals . . herself high watching over the hushed air Nazareth draw nearer.

Her body is tall, dizzily, to herself. It bears her brow where lives the strength that bears her body along.

—I could faint. I reckon my body is weak.

Will you fall down now, that you have risen up?

But *I* am strong, John Cloud. Have no fear. I'll meet you at your height. . .

The last smooth mile. She sees the pier out-thrust into the bay. She sees the paintless houses of her town clutching the unkempt brow of the hill. —Shame, shame!

Her breast is dry with the horror of the shame of the dead life of her world.

—I'll burn you clean. All of you: all of us. We'll equal the pitiless sun! . . .

Sand veers. Sand is the cheek of a god who laughs. The pier juts shakily. It reaches no place: an impotent gesture, the pier. The sand shifts up . . a terrene laughter: she is grim with it. —My body is weak, I am strong. Her feet stride fast. The sand flanks nauseously sidewise. The pier waves in the air like the antenna of a bug crushed into the clay by the heel of a god.

Your lips, John, cannot touch my lips, they can burn with fire of mine! . . .

Earth is a pool of murky dissolutions. The bay lies dead. The sun droops over the earth, and the houses of Nazareth lie cold like the ashen corpse of a fire. Only her brow is high. . .

Part Four

DUSK

THEY are coming out of the Revival Tent. The preacher's rasp has scaled its height and fallen. They flutter to their feet, lean drab-clothed men and women: from their throats the buzzing voices swarm toward the common note. Opulent words of love and faith are pushed by their thin voices up into the air. The Deacon has made his announcements: —Church goes on. Time falls with all its glittering prohibitions into the drab eternity of Church. His voice is high. Gloating and rebuke waft his stale messages of meetings, sewing circles and collection with a voice as verdant as the words of the preacher who has a voice that rasps. "You should have heard me more," goes with the Deacon's voice. And they are coming out from the

Revival Tent. The preacher has rasped his climax, he is tumbling down. Brave words of faith and love have been high wafted out of leaden throats. Eager eyes, voices almost fierce have asserted the victory of meekness, helped the preacher hoist them . . *rasp rasp frenzy, rasp up, rasp eye, blood, passion up* . . to the release of vision: love there, love allowed, rasp up to love allowed. And they are coming out from the Revival Tent. The rasp of the preacher has not hoisted them quite: high words lead-winged have not hoisted them quite. There for a spell they dangled, off the Nazareth ground, the choked tent and their vision off the ground; yet under the free sweet spaces of the Lord his rasping and their own song-words jerked them toward. Not quite. There they suspended . . *rasp rasp up up* . . there they strained . . *lift me a bit a bit more heft to that pull* . . there they stayed . . *rasp rasp rasp rasp DOWN*. . . They are coming out of the Revival Tent. Sluggish blood not whipped to foam. Clottish blood shutting out sun and making their faces sallow, hard . . *blood should foam, blood should flood.* . . They are coming clottish thick from the Revival Tent: and the preacher has failed.

—God ain't so easy to reach like He used to be. Y' don't ketch on to His bootstraps easy, no mo'. Got to h'ist yo'self up, nowadays, by yo' own bootstraps.

Men and women, boys and girls come out. A remnant lingers. The preacher subdued is speaking to them yet. *They* ain't so hard to h'ist up. His voice rasps less. His little yellow eyes glow thankfully. His smile dwells on the Remnant who stay, who have been h'isted up. —Nothing else counts. The Remnant. I am the Remnant. His little paunch is rounder as his round hands clasp it, and the yellow eyes warm out upon his Remnant. His voice is different: thin like a paper strip, but waxen smooth, now he no longer strives to make of it a banner of the Lord across the Southern skies. He chats colloquially to the clustered Remnant: familiar with them (he does not know he has failed): familiar with God (—I am God's and God can't fail. If God chooses only a Remnant, *I* cannot fail). He chats. But under the warming beam of his eyes a glance, furtive and fearful, vaults the little group who press about his pulpit, takes in the long rows of wooden emptiness whence Nazareth has drifted from the Tent: and in even measures, harsh and cold, the benches speak their word to the wistful glance covert within his eyes. His lips purse and his voice a little rasps once more, glowing a benison upon the Remnant.

Men, the solid men of Nazareth, mark and support the crowd that forms at the Tent's mouth. It is a clot of tangential pressures held together. It shuttles in and out upon itself. It is hard with words and intercourse of gesture. It is the Town of Nazareth pressing upon itself for an eye, for a direction. There are tall lean men silk-haired, cadaverous, whose words come hard like steel pins. There are heavy men with flaring brows and the mustachios of musketeers whose words are a roar. There are men with sallow eyes not looking; there are men with ripe red lips, too ripe. . . Men make the structure of the outlet crowd. The women stand and shred among them, pale light beams, emanant escapes of the hard male hungers. Men dry as bone, vacillant stiff like autumn grass, men lush and hard like the salt marshes baked by the sun: and their women among them, disembodied, making in their separate wistfulness the duality of Nazareth that is its Law.

The edge of the crowd shifts, flutters. It is the place of the women. A solid clot the center where the men talk affairs. But the affairs they talk, the opalescent gossip of the women are feelers of atoms nostalgic to be close. The substance that bulged the Tent mourns for its dwindling unity. Under the sky, solidity runs out and clots afresh: words rustle, hands clasp, eyes hold, that the substance of the Tent live longer.

—Fo' yo' ain't h'isted us up. *Rasp Rasp.* Yo' ain't h'isted us away!

It is tumescence cheated. In the mass threatened with dispersal lives still the glow that should have come to flame.

—What is God for? Jesus, what are you for?

—Ain't it a shame God's got so hard to git holt on?

Nazareth lingers, dangerously half-roused: in its soul's dark smolder a sore spot that is fire.

—It is time to die.
It is time to be gettin home.
Let the spark that mustn't catch glim out.

—It is time to die.
Always, it is time to die.
Birth is a sin, and sun is a mocking sin.

—Sun . . sun . . eternal Orgasm,
What more do you want?
Myriad men sparks make you:
Glowing women make you.
Where is the Lord that'll h'ist us up to Him?

—The sun don't care.
O no!
He sucks my men, he sucks my women white.
Sun laughs!
I'm cheated by white sky. . .

. . But they smile at each other:
holding together still: loth to let go and die.

"A good sermon."

"Well, that's over."

"O yes, pretty good."

"Now the Reverend Mack, *he* was good."

"What's become of him?"

"Why, he's dead, Mrs. Brewster. Done died last year. . ."

"You don' say! My! So young. He was fine, that parson."

"Overdid himself, Ah reckon. Broke a bloodvessel in his brain, a-preachin'."

"Too much thinkin'."

"Pretty good sermon, after all."

"Well, that's over."

"Will you be comin' round, George, after supper?"

"Reckon I might."

"Then says I to her: Why, my dear, you're a married woman!"

"Doesn't she think folks has eyes?"

"Nor ears. Why, what I heard by the South Gully!"

"They're sending an Orficer down, Bast tells me."

"No: you won't find *that* in the Gazette."

"Come roun' and I'll give you mine. O a fiver should do."

"No, Stoughton. The assessment's ten, this year."

"Everything goes up . . goes up . . even Revenoo Orficers."

"Now, if we could elect a President."

"Dey's nothin' but niggers up No'th."

"Sure. Pretty good. Now, the Reverend Mack."

"They oughtn't to allow 'em to have Revival."

"Het 'em up too durn much."

"Willoughby came round shoutin'."

"We'll tar him, ef."

"Nothin' but Voodoo drunk, that's all it is."

"Well, why shouldn't Peters stay on? He's fair. He's played fair. . ."

"The assessing of that turpentine grove by Lounsville."

"O they is alright."

"Yes indeed, Ma'am. Good evenin' to *you,* Ma'am."

"Splendid sermon."

"Now, the Reverend Mack."

"O couldn't ha' been better."

"Dignified."

"What we needs."

"Mind talks nowadays."

"And yet. . ."

. . Voices thickly dryly twine a straw tangle through the slow mass moving up to Main Street; angular bodies bowing faint gesticulant sharp pent jets of easelessness at play up out from the horizontal pace to Main Street; maze of eye-seek, lip-curl, finger-twist-and-jerk within the sluggish forward of the way to Main Street; choked breast, clamped heart-leap, gnaw of the spark a cancer in their brains throb shuttle thresh deliberate slow to Main Street: HALT

Virginia Hade

She stands at ease in the center of the street. Her white height thrusts its red heart at them. Athwart her head, the town fades: they feel the stroke of her eyes. Staccato roofs, porches on piles drag to the right, lurch to the left . . are gone. She, hard and sure, stands and is real. On her brow they see a smudge of blood. And in her hand upheld, they see a knife.

The crowd compresses upon itself. She watches her work as terror and amaze wipe blandness from eyes, inject an angular rush upon these somnolent muscles. Terror and amaze cover eyes an instant and are gone. Mist of stirring: a release faint and hopeful curls like a first flame in the mass of Nazareth. She sees now freedom and gladness.

She is at ease with her hard eyes blacksmiling, while her magic works.

The crowd breaks into integrate parts. It is a crowd maturing. From its hearty will eyes muscles limbs are fleshed: with a young joy muscles and limbs move to the creating of its will. Judge Hade and Bob Hade step from the crowd. They come up to Virginia.

The father places his hands upon her arms. But she is firm, resting in the magic of her work.

Bob Hade takes the knife from her hand.

He looks at it: and from that instant he looks at his sister no more. He clasps the knife as if it were some absolute deep Thing making his sister dim.

He is alive with a nervous luminous glow. He turns to the crowd, he is the crowd's sharp spirit: he is the culminant word of the crowd grown to voice. His lips move freely, tasting their masterful words. And from his eyes comes a splendor as of revelation.

"Men," his voice is mellow. "Men . . this knife . . I know this knife. John Cloud."

He does not lift his voice. He does not urge. His words are free. They have wings. They have faith. They bear with them a glamorous life all dawning. They career, sure of themselves, low-planing to the ears of the men who hear them.

The crowd is a birth of colors interwhirled. Murmur and suspense and hunger flush the dim crowd to life. It moves upon itself: fertile, condign. It breaks out fluently from its drab smolder. It opens, passionate, giving out its men: giving the wealth of its substance.

Men part from the crowd's vague, moving in vibrancy across the space (the sun lifts the clay into red oscillant tremors) to where the two men and the girl stand sheer. Like blood, men rise from the crowd's belly to the crowd's high head. Boys pale and tense with lips that curl; mature young men stoop-shouldered, necks craned stiff; heavy men hunched on themselves; hard men whose wills impressed come out in the flint of their eyes. They are the substance of Bob Hade's words. They join the words of the Head. The crowd stands living in its Head. They move, they go forth spreading sure and at work, the words of the Head.

The men have scattered: no true scattering. The men have gone forth from the crowd like its will, like hands of a body to reach for certain tangible things.

Virginia stands alone beside her father, Bob is gone. He looks at her. The men and the crowd, after the look that kindled them, see her no more. She leans a little on her father's arm. A little thought lies crooked in her mind, that if she had a mother he could now be with the men.

A buckboard clatters up: the mules prance: they too are of the dawning ecstasy.

The wood of the wagon gleams in the sun.

"Better step in, daughter."

Only her father is a soft discord in the steel lilt of the world.

"Come." It is a mother's firmness. "Come. I'll help you home."

She steps forward free of her father's arms. She sees him.

"Must I go home?"

"Yes, daughter. Come."

From the distance, the scattered men draw in again. Boys tense-lipped carry rope. Heavy men carry slender guns. All are sure, all are laved in a glum rhythm as of a dawn scarce broken and yet certain to rise and to spread.

Virginia sees them. A smile touches her face: it is a smile of gentle reminiscence. And its touch upon her eyes and lips is like a whip on them. Her face contorts. She sees her father there.

"Father," she says. "I'm all right." Her

hand is at her breast. "A bit of a wound." —*Stay here!*

"Daughter, step in."

"Father, stay here!" —Why do I want him here?

They do not mind her. She has brought to them what now these boys and men and women carry like a love, sinister gay, above their heads as they cluster, as they plan. Rope, guns and knives of the men are one with the draw of the women's eyes, with the glint of the women's words.

Virginia steps into the buckboard. She steps in slow and heavy: the mules prance away.

The men form a knot apart. They confer with their white brows clustered.

The Tent flaps debile. It is empty. Nazareth is empty. The crowd has drawn unto itself all of the Tent, all of Nazareth.

But the men are apart. They are an organ thrust forth from the crowd. They are bleak and dark. They do not glow and exclaim like the crowd itself. They are silent, muttering low. They are a promise: a larval joy. The crowd . . women, children, old men, sick men . . look on the knot of men with their ropes and guns, and love its darkling ugliness. It is an instrument for them of joy and of flame.

From the Tent's flapping mouth a little man appears. He is black-frocked. He stands a moment in the droop of canvas which he has tried to swell with the word of Christ: his eyes wince as he catches the crowd's dark note. His hands flutter before him. He rushes with pattering feet to the knot of men.

"Men! Brothers!" he butts against them shrilling. "What are you going to do? What are those guns for, brothers? You have just come from Christ. What are those guns?"

Backs fend him off. His hands whimmer.

This larval knot must burst in its own time.

He turns. He is a little sleek plump man. His eyes blink, he suffers. With whimmering hands, he is drawn away from the knot of men . . into the men-drained crowd. Flutter and press of women take him in, make him theirs. In saccade fragments, women's phrases agglutinate his will. His hands droop silent.

"I have done my duty."

Talk binds them close: the women who are one, waiting the stroke of the men.

—Dark hard engine: ugly: full of sweetness
    We wait for you.
Burst us open with your bursting flame-
        might
    We wait.
We murmur and talk, we cheat and lie,
Our hands upraised in protest cheat and
        lie,

We are waiting. Burst us.
Our words cheat time, for we must wait:
We are waiting.

—Time and suspense we cover.
(That's what the protest's for,
That's what the words and gestures and
the screams
Serve): Serve us!
We are waiting.

—We'll rouse you!
With resistance.
With the resisting word and the resisting
hand to touch and fire your passion,
Ugly men!
Larval pushing men!
Burst us. We are waiting.

For the men have made a rope of themselves. Bob Hade is the head. He strides and the men are a rope, taut, writhing after. Thick men and lean men and callow youths, strange to their first ecstasy, rope out and are away toward Niggertown.

The crowd remains: *—Burst us. We wait.*

TOWARD Niggertown.

The earth rolls back beneath their feet: Niggertown closer. The road is a gash in the earth: thc banks of the road, red, grass-fringed, roll behind. The trees lean back, roll back: the squat frame houses come forth their moment, blink, roll on in the encompassing maze of the processioned trees. Niggertown . . earth rolling back and trees a slow procession overhead . . Niggertown close.

The road narrows. Houses, as they come now from the film ahead and flash their moment into the film behind, are lowlier and stained with a dubious question. Hinterland is here: the limbo world between the white and the black . . what lives in this gray is gray with a dubious question. Earth rolls: tree marge nearer: cotton field in the beginning dusk, orchard and corn and cane brake veer like rigid triangles shifted on a plane, pivoting past from the slow harsh rope of men . . Bob Hade's the head . . bearing snakewise into Niggertown.

The cypress trees spring up, clasp their fingers under sky, arch back. It's the swamp. It's the nigger-swamp. The man snake slides.

Boys youth men . . part of a livid rope. Feet shuffle, manifold feet of boys youth men. Feet strike in dissonance on clay. Feet patter as feet strike in scatter of time. Feet thud as they crowd together . . spread again. But one pace ever, deeper than the splinternote of feet on the raveling ground. One pace is this pace of purpose, it has its being above the plethora of feet . . in the shoulders of the men pushing, in the eyes of the men fixed beyond. All one this engine. The breakpelt of feet is a band of pied hard colors under the One, under the man rope snaking to Niggertown.

Black child-face peers . . burns an instant in the dusk . . has vanished. From the window frames of cabins through the glaze of the glass hot faces gaze, dark faces rigid in fear. There is a cry: a woman's heart visioning life, this bitter ruthless Thing. Faces are gravid with their sight. Eyes start, mouths mutter. Man rope snakes on.

A white snake twists: black wake of rigid limbs, arms up . . "Lo'd!" . . palms outstretched beneath the careless sky. A white snake twists.

Minds of men make it. Young and old: tender men, iron men, men with brains of straw, men leather-skinned, men with harsh palates, and men subtle in whose eyes this cypress world becomes a tortured dance—trees twining anguished under the ash-red sky.

They are a rope twisting, a rope pushing. The world of niggerlife is pushed from their white drouth. The minds making the march displace the world whose tangent fragments scream on their obtuse sense. Fragments of mouth, eyes, palm from niggerworld stand sculpted in terror and are splintered off. Nothing is real save the man rope twisting. Nigger horror . . dim. Nigger prayer asmolder in the secret cabin air . . whiffed away. Virginia is a spoken word . . is gone. John Cloud is a name not yet born to its moment. All ravels up . . all pushes behind. The white rope twists eternal, moveless there under the moving sky. And the cypress branches pass: and the answering wails of the awakened town wail away: and the red earth folds.

White man rope, rope of white man minds pure of all thought . . pure of all outwardness: *One* in the moveless black will of its march.

THE Revival Tent flaps in the low sun. It is filled with emptiness. Long shadows point across its new-pine rails. It is a naked vernal sepulcher . . sweet-smelling pine, sweet-smelling dust of the pine . . and it is empty, stripped now of its benches.

The Square before the Tent is shaded from the sun by the cross-street roofs. Up to Main Street the road is a wine-hued tongue. And it is full of bustling human words: and it is full of song of expectation.

The benches stripped from the Tent of God . . here they are, larding the Square. Benches of mourners and of worshipers. Here they stand gay, stand expectant: all fresh new pine. They have become these smiling open rows: and they wreathe in wide semicircles on the Square: and they face, holding in the embrace of their round gaze, a solitary tree.

It is a cottonwood. From a low branch the leaves and shoots have been plucked. It stands blackpointing with its naked limb toward the gay wreathe of benches.

The crowd takes seat, gets up, shifts into groups, murmurs, confers. It has a bloom of peace. There is no laughter, there is no high pitched voice. No person moves beyond the sedateness of a walk. But in the thrust of heads, in the peer and jet of eyes toward the rising ground where the white man rope has vanished, there is dance.

Nazareth waits. Nazareth waits in a mute gay dance. The benches plucked from the gloom of the Tent wreathe in a waiting smile. The tree, with its nude branch, stands and points up waiting.

—*Upon the black branch of the black tree let there be Fruit!*
Let there be seed, let there be fruit for my passion!

MARY CARTIER stands in her cabin door. She knows these footsteps through the stir of leaves. She is at the cabin gate. The moving from door to gate has made no trace upon her mind. —It is John! Slow footsteps steady. —John like always. John whole!

Since John went away . . "I'll be back sho, Mary" . . since John went and since Miss Hade was here, John and strange Miss Virginia in a whirl of blood and a black dance of white men all about John's eyes . . weaving a web of death about my eyes! Here he is. His steady pace, *that is John!* And the sun's just dropped from the green hollow. *That is John!* See . . sun holds up a copper finger yet. What are the ghosts of fear against this: John is coming. *That is John!*

John's feet speak straight: speak close. His body from the shadow is word: "All's good."

—O the bad dance in my mind was a dream, was a dream.

He closes the gate . . so slow . . and then his hands are hers.

"Mary, Ah's come back."

She looks at his hands . . thumb cut? O nothing that . . and draws them close so she can see his eyes.

His eyes. . .

—Walk lies and body walking straight is a lie!

She looks into his eyes. They meet her bravely. Beneath their bravery is a bleeding. Beneath their caress . . —he loves me! . . lies a question to which he has no answer. Fear grips her, strains her to the narrow question deep like a wound within his eyes.

"John!"

"Ah said I'd come back. An' I did. Here I am, Mary."

"John?"

But he can say no more. What is this bleeding? How can she get at that? Her daze presses her down. Her hands hold his in a frantic pressure that stifles out all thought.

"Thah's trouble, Mary. Thah's goin' to be trouble."

"John!"

"At Pine Cliff, 'twas. I don' understand. But Ah reckon it was true. It happened. . . Miss Hade——"

He swallows heavily, and through the smile that hides his eyes a black bewilderment like a black blood floods.

—He has said it. *Trouble.* You have heard it. *Trouble.* You have heard it. *Trouble.* Not a dream!

Her hands, still holding his, rise to her

breasts and it is his hands she presses to herself.

A doubt is in her. But she feels his palms so quiet on her breasts. Doubt dies. His hands are sleeping on her breasts? So still they are. —Let me hold them there. The first time . . and the last?

There is a quiet moment. His hands, miraculously still, grow to be her flesh, to be her breasts. All of his high strength is flesh of her. —He has not sinned against me! Mary knows, without word further, the rightness of what John did at Pine Cliff. But she knows: life has given her this hour, this dawn and dusk made one . . she knows how death was born there. Ruin wreathes from that hid moment she will never see to all that she will ever look upon. Wreathes all about her world its gray ash garlands, binding in death this dawn and this dusk of their love.

—He has come. Bringing the last hour with the first.

She lifts his two hands sleeping from her breasts. She gazes at them. She shakes her head . . as an old woman might.

"John," she whispers. "Hurry! Don't go home. Run! Back country! Quick!"

He looks at her. He looks away and looks at her again. He shakes his head.

"There's nothin', Mary, why I should run away."

"O there is, John!"

"There's nothin', Mary."

"There's death."

Her voice is clear in the dim day: "O I know, Heart. O I know, Boy! There is no reason. But I love you, John. Yo' ain't goin' to die, my Honey, when I loves you?"

He clasps her shoulders.

"I love you, Mary."

They are washed clear of doubt. They are washed clear of struggle.

"You must go!"

He shakes his head, and smiles. His eyes fall back into a sort of slumber.

"No. . . There's nothin', Mary, why I ken run away." . .

These footfalls too she knows, though she has never heard their like before.

John stands, facing Mary, facing away from the gate, facing the cabin of Mary. A woman with feet crowding, fumbling, broken in their hurry, falls through the gate and kneels before her son.

"John—quick! Honey! Mah only God-gift. *Fo' me!* Run, John. Ah knows yo' is clean. Da's why. Run—fo' me! Fo' Mary, John. Not fo' me, den. Fo' Mary. Run, John!"

She is on her knees beside the upright girl, before her son. And John stands firm.

The leaf stir stills. Through the dusk the measured march of many men like a cold beating pulse, like a slow tiding flood, moves up, moves up. The footfalls strike articulate the earth. The trees shrink in, draw their stilled leaves away. March. March. The stroke of the feet, a beating iron pulse, ribs from the ground solid like trunks of moving magic trees. It is a march of trees. Iron-trunked, white-leafed, marching shattering trees! . . . Halt.

John has not moved. At his shoulder, facing the gate stands Mary: at his feet, with rigid arms, his mother kneels. They have not moved.

John turns.

The men are grouped about the gate and the rail. In the dull light their forms stand like an iron paling.

Bob Hade steps out. He flings the gate wide open, bursting its feeble butt.

"John Cloud," he says. "Come on. We want you."

John stands still. From the rigor of the group, eyes glint, mouths tensely mutter, hands stir with weapon and rope. John stands still. On Bob Hade's face a sneer harms the peace of his will.

"Did you think, Cloud, them two nigger women'd save you?"

A tremor in John's face dies down. He is all strong. His voice is stone. He says:

"You know better, yo'self, than to think I grouped 'em there."

His words, cold and flinchless, strike in a single blow against the group of men.

They are man and youth and man. A subtle rotting threatens the Rope, threatens the Iron Paling: threatens to make them men with eyes to see this quiet straight man and his molten women. . .

—She is lovely. That breast is in pain. I
have lain in such a breast.
*Save me, Rope! Save me from that
bitter longing.*

—He looks honest. He looks clean. Perhaps it is I who am wrong.
High steel spikes of my Pride
Save me from being wrong!
Save me from feeling low!

—What do we know? Whom have we asked? Ask him.
What can a nigger answer
When we ask for blood?

—She is a mother too. Mammy o' mine, you'd have such arms around me
If they hunted me.
Can I go back to you?
No; I can blot you out.

—But she is lovely, young. It's she he loves. They love each other.
There might be a mistake.
No mistake this: I can't touch your black breast!
No mistake this: I can't touch your deep song!

—ROPE: SAVE ME ROPE
SPIKE ME AROUND IN SAFETY, IRON FENCE
FENCE OF HATE SAVE ME
FENCE OF HATE SHUT OUT THAT FLOOD
CUP OF DEATH, COOL ME
COOL ME, STEEL. . .

Bob Hade comes forward. He is their last word.

"Come on." The crisis is behind him of the Rope that almost turned to man and youth and man. But his words are pale. "Come on."

"What do you want?"

"We want you . . and quick. Will you come peaceful, nigger? Or should we step in and fetch you?"

John feels the storm of his mother's suppliance about to break. His hand on her head presses peace, entreaty of peace.

"Stay where you are. I'll come. . . Mother," he looks down at her head. Her face is hidden. "Mammy, let Mary take you home. I'll jes' go, honey, an' speak with these here men."

Hade's sneer runs through them.

"Yo'll come . . an' yo'll shut yo' mouth. We don' want none of yo' words. It's you, we want."

John strokes his mother's head. He makes a step. His mother falls in a faint across his feet. He does not look at his mother: he does not look at Mary. He goes forth in a stern possession, avoiding his mother's body: with his eyes slumbrous and his lips parted as if he kissed the air.

Mary has not moved. Her eyes turn, moving alone, upon her lover. He stands among the men: taller and calm like stone. They swarm around him, maggoting his clearness. They shuffle his arms in rope, they halter his head: they swallow him up. Only his haltered head is free and is high above them.

Mary's eyes move with his moving, fixed

in the chanting lull of his disappearance. . .

She is alone. At her feet, the mother-flesh of him who has gone forever. Her eyes are far away for they have gone with him who is gone. Her body is dead, for her eyes are far away and know not her body, know not herself, know not yet the pain of this one knowing she has: that he is borne away who is her love and that the bitter Thing which is, which this is, which remains: is Life.

VIRGINIA lies in her bed. Her eyes are open, she is on her back. The day outside is waning hot: sun from the simmering bay sends its shafts horizontal to her shuttered room. She feels her room clear, herself dim. The bed is a wide low frame of mahogany: its headpiece flares and the Hade shield stands flanched above her pillow. The sheet that covers her is smooth. Shadow blues its soft-washed linen pallor. The blinds to the balcony are shut. A gray coolth lies about her wide-eyed: it enwraps the *Empire* lowboy, makes the rag rug gleam less upon the black wood floor: it dims the shimmer heap of her silk undergarments on the little stool. The curtains of blue chintz are gray with the dusk. Only her desk between the curtained windows remains bright. The blotter is pink: and on the blotter between two candlesticks lies a book. It is leather-tooled, bright blue: a book of verse . . *Lilies in Arcady* picked out in gold . . and it is by her good and courteous friend, Herman Shreve, the Charleston poet, who wants her for his wife.

The room is cool against the torrid day: fending her well from the day. The room is gentle against the torrid storm: afloat and aloof with its quiet pretty things fending her well. Through the slits of the drawn blinds, the light burns in, is broken, casts on the farther wall a gleam of stripes against dusk peace. Lying in her bed Virginia hears the murmur that has dwelt in Nazareth since the moment . . far like a far thing seen through an inverted telescope . . when she stood in Nazareth Square. It comes to her broken and removed like the striped day on the farther wall of her room. It is a murmur dry and thirsting: a murmur low with expectancy. Since she stood upon the

Square, it has filled like the heat the air of Nazareth.

—But my room is cool.

—It is below. It will rise, that murmur, to a howl. It does not faint. It persists . . . murmur murmur. It does not spend itself. It is hardy and sure and slow. It waits. Am I waiting too? Am I a part of it?

She lies within her sheet. —I am still. No murmur in me. I am the creator! She is at peace, she is filled. No murmurous thirst is she, waiting, crouching. Hers is peace filled and silent.

She lies at ease within her bed. She watches a toe thrust up within the sheet.

—What am I going to do?

She is concerned in her own quiet. —Why am I not waiting also? Why am I so quiet? But she knows she is not waiting. She is replete. She can stir a toe and watch it lift the linen. She can brush a fly from her moist hair. She can think: My hair drugs you, fly? The murmur of Nazareth murmurs: she who brought it to be is outside and is still.

—I who made it can stop . . what they are waiting for.

She knows this, lying quiet in her sheet: naked within her gown within her sheet.

She knows this less: —Did I make it? Dare I stop what I did not create?

But if she goes, if she pleads . . she alone . . she can save John Cloud!

—Will I go? . . And what is "saving"? . . And what is "John Cloud"?

The sheet, a little moist, presses on the cotton on her wound. —Who made this wound? My hand. Yet it is your wound, John.

—Will I go?

She knows not what is the heart, who is the goal and prey of the deep murmur. —Am I down there? Am I *your* victim,

John? You made this wound which your hands did not touch, which you know nothing of. Did you make the storm of Nazareth that hunts you? make it to hunt you? make me make Nazareth hunt you?

Murmur. Murmur.

—We understand . . what?

The murmur of Nazareth suddenly claps to stillness. She watches her toe lift the soft sheet.

—Will I go?

From her toe up to her eyes, her body lives. —That is me! Will my body rise? Will it rise and dress itself and go? Will it kill this murmur that is gone, this ominous silence risen from the murmur?

—Will I go?

She feels the snakelike mob move back with its prey within the waiting Square. John is bound and haltered. He walks enmeshed . . solitary. Within the wreath of Nazareth a tree and a bare branch.

Silence.

What lives in this silence? It is gravid and hot. What truth will it bring forth?

HOWL

The shutters of her room shiver:

HOWL

. . bursts in her room.

Chairs, gay bright desk, gay blue poetry book, the light stripes on the wall shiver and dance in the howl that is Nazareth in voice . . Nazareth in fruit at last.

Virginia lies in her bed beneath her pallid sheet. And her toe presses up.

—Will I go?

THE MOB is on him. He is ripe: they have him.

Tall lovely nigger. Nigger clean, nigger brave, nigger full of the meat of beauty. What a morsel!

The men work fast. Day dims and torches cast their lacerant glare on the tall tree. John Cloud stands nude. Torchlight and the glow of the gone sun eat upon his body, lip its bronze to dancing shimmer.

The women crowd the benches, grasp the benches as if a great wave rocked them: as if a wave menaced to cast them prone upon the naked man. They throw their passion in the air and it falls at the torch-burst tree. Women shriek, women laugh, women weep. A little black-frocked man bobs from the flock of women and his white hands dance.

"O Christ . . O Christ!"

His face is blenched. His voice is a straw cast away on the combers of the mob rolling down, breaking at the torch-burst tree.

The men work fast. Dusk heavies. Blossoms of torch flare and wave and spurt. Fire-seeds of torch scatter to the tree's top leaves, to the farthest quaking tier of the mob. Fire-seed, foam and comber of voice, whirr of mob and an ominous low rustle as men work, drag wood, drag rope . . couch the Square sinking into dark, draw the Square in and down to the fragile central point where a man stripped stark stands up beneath a tree.

The men work fast. Day glooms. Day dies. The Square sinks into a well of night. A rope whips taut. A body dangles in air. A body dangles in flame.

Nazareth is sinking with the Square . . man jerks up . . with the world sinks Nazareth into the well of night. The well of night wells up. Nazareth plunges down.

Only the body of a man, in the air, stays unmoved.

About him flame. Beneath him night. Beneath him Nazareth.

Fair bronze body melting in the fire.

. . . . . .

The fire tongues fall back from the charred body of John Cloud.

Nazareth beneath him peers with grimed eyes through the murk of its spent lust.

Virginia, soothed by the silence, sleeps in her bed.

The *Psyche* stands at the empty pier that points from Nazareth out into the world.

1920–1922.

The University of Illinois Press
is a founding member of the
Association of American University Presses.

University of Illinois Press
1325 South Oak Street
Champaign, IL 61820-6903
www.press.uillinois.edu